… was born in Chicago, Illinois, but … New York. A graduate of Radcliffe College, she has received both Guggenheim and Rockefeller grants for her work. Her first novel, *Love and Friendship*, was published in 1962. Her other publications include *The Nowhere City* (1965), *Imaginary Friends* (1967), *The War Between the Tates* (1974) and *Only Children* (1979), all of these have been published in Penguin. Her latest book is *The Language of Clothes* (1981).

Alison Lurie lives in upstate New York, where she teaches English at Cornell University.

Alison Lurie

Real People

Penguin Books

14872412

Penguin Books Ltd, Harmondsworth, Middlesex, England
Penguin Books, 625 Madison Avenue, New York, New York 10022, U.S.A.
Penguin Books Australia Ltd, Ringwood, Victoria, Australia
Penguin Books Canada Ltd, 2801 John Street, Markham, Ontario, Canada L3R 1B4
Penguin Books (N.Z.) Ltd, 182–190 Wairau Road, Auckland 10, New Zealand

First published in Great Britain by Heinemann 1970
Published in Penguin Books 1978
Reprinted 1983

Made and printed in Great Britain by
Richard Clay (The Chaucer Press) Ltd, Bungay, Suffolk
Set in Linotype Baskerville

0140045821

For Philip

Come what will, I cannot, when I write,
think always of myself and of what is
elegant and charming in femininity; it
is not on those terms, or with such ideas,
I ever took pen in hand: and if it is only
on such terms my writing will be
tolerated, I shall pass away from the
public, and trouble it no more.

CHARLOTTE BRONTË
Letters

Imagine a deserted estate in northern New England. Five hundred rolling acres, mainly forested with hemlock and white pine. Imposing stone gateposts; long sloping velvet lawns brocaded with the moving shadows of clouds; a thirty-five-room stone mansion in Victorian-baronial style; picturesque old stables and outbuildings; two Italian marble fountains, one indoors; three large artificial ponds stocked with fish and water lilies; and a once-famous rose garden.

It is fifty years since the last owners lived here. The fountains are silent; the main entrance to the mansion under the heavy portico is closed, and a line of large sharp rocks bars the drive. The shades are drawn in the forty-foot music room with its imported carved ceiling; the drawing-room furniture is shrouded in muslin. Behind the house the broad terrace above the lawn is bare except for red and green tendrils of vine advancing over cracked plaster and crumbling stone. No one walks there.

But Illyria (for this is the romantic name of the place) is not completely deserted. Though the owners are gone, there are ten or twelve 'guests' currently in residence, on extended visits of from a fortnight to several months. A lady named Mrs Kent has been appointed to look after these guests; and she is assisted by a secretary and a domestic staff of eight. If we could look through the stone walls of the mansion this morning, we would see them busy at work: making beds, polishing floors, going over the accounts; chatting together as they dust the statues and Edwardian bric-a-bac, repair the window screens, or

9

hull quarts of strawberries from the garden for tonight's shortcake.

The guests, by contrast, are all solitary, and seem either idle or worse. At ten AM each is shut in his room alone, either in the main house or in isolated cottages about the grounds. Two of them are staring out of their windows. Two others are pacing about restlessly. One writes a letter, and signs it with a false name, while another reads (without permission) somebody else's private correspondence. One is methodically bending a pile of his hosts' coat hangers out of shape; one is picking out discords on a grand piano; and one, apparently, is making love to himself.

June 29

At Illyria again. I've got my old room, with the big bay window looking out across the lawn, and the six-foot marble bathtub.

It's very beautiful here – heavenly. Even more so than I remembered. How could I forget? But one does, partially at least. Imprisoned in one's house, on some gritty gray winter day when the children are home from school with colds, it doesn't seem possible there could be such a place anywhere.

It was right to come back here; I had to come, whatever Clark thinks. I tried to explain, and Clark tried to understand, said he understood – but all the same he was irritable and chilly for days before I left, and I know from experience he'll be the same after I get back. Usually he claims I'm imagining things, or that he's depressed for some other reasonable reason, but this time he admitted it.

JANET: You're not cross about that meeting, or Bessie's bleaching your shirts; you're cross because I'm going to Illyria again.
CLARK: Well, naturally. I prefer to have you here.
JANET: But I am here, almost all the time.
CLARK: I'd like you to be here all the time.

If Janet wants a rest, he silently thinks, why can't she rest at home? The children are both in camp all day now, and Bessie can take care of the house. Or if she wants to write stories, why can't she write them at home as she used to?

I don't know why. Only that I can't.

It's not that I don't *write*, in the dictionary sense. I make notes of conversations and metaphors and ideas for plots until my journal runs over with them; I put sentences on paper and line them up into paragraphs and even pages. Only I can't fit the pages together so that they mean anything; by the time the children come home, my waste-basket is full of interrupted fragments and crumpled false starts. Since the book came out, more than six months ago, I've only managed to finish two very short stories; mere sketches really. And everything I do reminds me of something I've done before. Partly, of course, that's inevitable when one's been in the same place for fifteen years. Our life in Westford is really very uneventful, and most of what there is to be written about I have already written about.

I can't make Clark understand what it's been like for me this spring – that awful stale, weak, frightened feeling that comes over me when I'm shut up in my study, alone with the knife-edged stack of blank white paper, the sharpened yellow pencils, the typewriter holding up its dismembered black bits of words like some elaborate machine of torture. ('Listen, Janet Belle Smith,' they all say. 'You'd better talk, if you know what's good for you.') Everything in the room looks either threatening or false – even the fresh flowers in my blue enamel teapot, which seem alive but which I know are really dead.

When I try to describe it, Clark thinks I'm just indulging in nervous poetic exaggeration – because obviously, if it really bothered me that much, I would stay out of the study. ('I don't understand why you feel you have to keep on writing stories,' he said once, when I was particularly and conspicuously miserable. 'It seems to cause you mainly discomfort.')

And my belief that if I could get back to Illyria, to this room, things would begin to go right again, has always been incomprehensible to Clark, who can work anywhere (I've seen him open his briefcase and study papers from the office while eating breakfast, in taxis, on lurching crowded trains). Besides, he has never quite believed that people actually *work* here. First, because it looks like the most elegant sort of private hotel; and second, because writing stories or painting pictures simply isn't what he thinks of as work. Being an insurance executive is a serious occupation; writing, only a hobby (like the weekends he takes off sometimes to go bird watching with those people from Yale). An eccentric hobby; and in the long run rather an irritating one for a businessman's wife in a provincial city.

As for my idea that I can practice this hobby better in one room than another, he thinks that a pitiful illusion – and at times this spring I've been so low I almost acquiesced. But I don't now.

Perfect weather. But the weather's always perfect here: sun, rain, fog, wind, frost – they're all becoming to Illyria. Still, it's at its most characteristic best on a day like this. The sky sky-blue, light falling in abstract expressionist patterns through the pine branches, a slight breeze. Actually, it's not so much Heaven (which is intellectual and unimaginable) as a sort of Eden, where all practical problems and responsibilities have vanished.

And it's so wonderfully quiet. At home, there's always the telephone and the doorbell – Bessie will answer, but of course I hear the ring and wonder who it is. And whenever I raise my eyes, I notice something I ought to do something about: smudges on the wallpaper, that peculiar bill from the cleaners ... Or I start worrying about Bessie's bad back that she won't see the doctor for, Clarkie's troubles in school, and Clary's sulks and rudeness at home. Or Clark's sick headaches, which he saw the doctor for but still unaccountably has ... If I look out the window, I don't see a view; instead I'm reminded that the garage will need repainting soon, I must call White's Nursery about spraying the fruit trees, and we've simply got to have the Hodgdens over to dinner. And when I look back at my story, it's fallen apart again. I suppose the wonder really is not that I've had so much trouble working in Westford, but that I've been able to work there at all.

Haven't seen Caroline Kent or any of the other guests yet. A man who introduced himself as 'Charlie Baxter' met me at the Lodge. He's taking Paula's place while she has six weeks' vacation in Europe. Illyria without Paula – impossible! I thought, and he may have intuited, for he began at once apologizing for his inexpertness as a guide – while I kept assuring him that on my third visit I didn't need one. He's agreeable, personable even (forty-seven or forty-eight? tall and slim, blond forelock going gray). But there's something familiar, and indefinably sad, about him. Literary failure, perhaps? 'You won't have seen any of my recent stuff; it's poetry mostly,' he insisted, smiling. Indeed, I hadn't that I can recall.

Charlie Baxter reported that Paula is enjoying the art and architecture abroad, but 'very homesick.' Of course this is her home, and has been for twenty years. I remember her out at the pool last summer telling Kenneth and me how awful it was to be away from Illyria.

PAULA: At first it's *such* a relief not to have to worry about fire, or whether one of the help will get sick, or some new guest will turn out to be an alcoholic. (Well, I don't really mind so much about the alcoholics; I say to myself, 'Poor dear, he's a good artist all the same.') I'm almost glad to go; but when I get to New York, or even Boston, it's dreadful. So noisy, and so dirty. I look at the faces on the street or in the subway, and they're all unhappy and angry. And I think, well, no wonder, living *there*. Usually after about a week I can't bear it any more. I have to come back here, where people are normal.

Story idea: Paula in N.Y. Like a character out of some nineteenth-century utopian novel, time-machined into this century, rightly appalled. But then one would have to describe Illyria. Or some equivalent place – what? No.

There's only one Illyria, and though it's a wonderful subject, nobody will ever write about it. Because if they do (as Caroline Kent has somehow made clear), they can never come back.

It's true, people are nicer here. Released from the strains of ordinary life – domestic anxieties and irritations; financial, social and emotional competition – they relax and bloom like flowers. Everyone becomes gentler, more open to new ideas. (Rosemarie Beck: 'You see them the first day at dinner: suspicious, defensive, tight. Within twenty-four hours all that's gone.')

Of course people's characters can only be improved relatively. There are a few who even at Illyria become merely tolerable. While others, already likable, take on amazing sweetness and charm. Even Paula, who prefers to think the best of everyone, recognizes the distinction, and speaks of her favorites as Lovely People. ('Kenneth's a Lovely Person,' or, sometimes, '... a Real Person.') And she's literally right. At Illyria one becomes one's *real* self, the person one would be in a decent world.

After supper

It was a little hard having to go down to dinner alone tonight – the first time at Illyria that Kenneth hasn't been here. Of course, two years ago I didn't know Kenneth, or anybody. I hovered nervously in the hall upstairs, waiting for the gong to sound, among lamps and tables, over-dressed in fringed silk (wondering if *I* was overdressed), while three or four people passed through with only cool glances of curiosity. But Kenneth stopped when he saw me; he smiled, came over and introduced himself. In a few moments I felt I had known him for weeks.

Kenneth won't be here until tomorrow, though, and I had to descend the grand staircase under the stained-glass window alone. (Carson McCullers, I've heard, once hid in her room at dinnertime for almost a week.) There was a crowd of people I didn't know in the hall, from which Caroline Kent, elegant in brocade, detached herself to welcome me, cordially but not comfortingly, and make introductions. 'Charlie Baxter. Sally ...' something. Though I tried to stop them, the rest of the names passed through my head like jets, with an unintelligible roar. I smiled as well as I could manage, and shook hands.

But then one of the hands turned out to belong to Gerald Grass, the young poet I met on my first visit; and there was Theodore Berg from last summer; and in a few moments I was sitting between them at Caroline's table, feeling better again.

I'm not as awed now as I was once. The dining room at Illyria is still an impressive place, with its polished dark oak furniture and wainscoting, red brocade wallpaper, crystal chandeliers and displays of antique silver – and Caroline Kent is an impressive woman. Antique-silver hair, red brocade dress, crystal-chandelier voice. And it's not only, or even mainly, that she matches the room. The way she sits in her chair, the motion with which she smooths the napkin across her knees, suggest unimaginable perfection of control. As Julius Goldstein commented last summer, Caroline probably hasn't put her elbows on the table, or even imagined putting them on the table, for sixty years.

But I know the rules now. One sits at Caroline's table one's first evening here, again on the last evening, and often enough in between to be polite. There's a special style of behavior there – everyone wipes his mouth more often and more tactfully, and takes smaller bites. Above all, there's a special style of conversation: a kind of formal jocularity, light-hearted but (in some hands at least) heavy-handed. I've never hear anything like it outside of Illyria, but I've read it in books – the humorous scenes in Edith Wharton, or early James. There are certain prescribed subjects: local history, geography, botany and meteorology; and news (but not scandal) of former guests.

The names of writers, artists and musicians who have never been here aren't mentioned.

Partly because Caroline is deaf, so that we must all speak unnaturally loud, this talk has a marked theatrical tone. It's as if we were improvising dialogue to suit the room – trying to echo the witticisms and compliments uttered there fifty or sixty years ago by the painters and poets to whom the Moffats first extended their hospitality. Or possibly it's their spirits who are ventriloquizing through us. Which would account for the fact that, once I've left the dining room, it's a real effort to remember anything we said. (But I suppose it's a good exercise to try.)

TEDDY: You certainly picked the right day to come, Janet. Our own strawberries and shortcake for dessert tonight! Isn't that so, Caroline?

CAROLINE: Yes. That's right.

JANET: Strawberry shortcake, oh my! How did you know?

TEDDY: (winking) I have my methods.

I still play the tune a little artificially; Teddy does it effortlessly, and with apparent enjoyment – but then, he's been coming to Illyria for over twenty years. I like him, though he's rather formidable – the more so because he doesn't at first seem it. To look at, he's a small, fat, unprepossessing elderly man with the face of an effeminate drunken cherub. But the high color is due only to high blood pressure, and Teddy is one of the most famous living American composers.

GERRY: I know what it is. He sneaks around and makes up to Mrs Akins.

CAROLINE: Oh, I don't think so.

Gerry improvises his dialogue even less well than I, though he looks the part perfectly. Young, very large, and poetically handsome in a Charles Dana Gibson way: noble brow, long curly fair hair and beard – rather like a great golden retriever in a psychedelic paisley shirt and leather vest. Undine Moffat would have adored him, and probably forgiven his stylistic errors more easily than Caroline does. She quite evidently didn't like the suggestion that people might interrogate the help behind her back. Nor did Teddy, who became rather waspish.

TEDDY: I do not. I have an infallible system *you* couldn't even guess at.

GERRY: I wouldn't want to know. I mean, that takes all the excitement out of it.

Gerry lost his East Village cool, grew a little hot and incoherent as he went on to make a speech in favor of the unexpected in life, with illustrative quotations from his own poems.

GERRY: ... I mean, like, 'Flowers exploding. Five-foot monkeys arriving on Greyhound buses.' That's what you want.

TEDDY: Very elegantly expressed. From your *Wet Dreams*, I think?

GERRY: Yeah.

TEDDY: But I believe you've quoted the line wrong. 'Five-foot monkeys fucking on Greyhound buses,' wasn't it?

GERRY: Uh, yeah.

Gerry's published work is as frank as any modern poet's, which of course is saying a good deal. When I heard him read at Trinity, I think he used every four-letter word there is; and nobody protested. But the social rules on obscenity have been reversed since I was in college. A writer can now print, or declaim in a public hall, lines he would hesitate to utter in ordinary society.

While dinner was going on, I was trying to identify the guests at the other tables. (The list in the mail room tells who's coming to Illyria each summer, but not when. Of the twenty or thirty names on it, some may have already left; others won't arrive until after I'm gone myself. I recognized one of them almost at once. That plain, dowdily dressed, but somehow distinguished old woman, with a roll of gray hair pinned to her head, next to Charlie Baxter – was H. H. Waters! (What luck for me.) With Charlie and Miss Waters were two people I couldn't identify: a pale, intellectual-looking man in his forties; and a muscular younger man with a red shirt, quite attractive, who laughed and moved around a lot. Conversation at this table was lively; I would have liked to be there. The other table was less interesting: only the dark, rather intense-looking girl I met earlier (Sally something) and a stocky young man.

Later

I went up to my room after supper, feeling so good that I thought I would try to write. But it was too late in a long day, and the warm breeze through the window, the sounds of voices off, kept fluttering the paper in my typewriter distractingly. So, as Teddy had suggested, I joined him on the lawn by the tennis court, where we sat on a rustic bench and watched the end of the croquet game. A scene out of Eakins or Winslow Homer: great pines on all sides; thick turf across which the declining sun cast stripes of gold and green plush; the shiny varnish and bright paint of the croquet mallets and balls; and the four men in their light-colored summer clothes, standing about the lawn in varied attitudes.

The game was more interesting than I'd expected. They've been taking it seriously this summer, and play every evening after supper.

TEDDY: Croquet's become veryvery intense this year. Quite symbolical.

JANET: Symbolical of what?

TEDDY: Oh, everything. Luck in general; male potency, possibly. But mainly artistic success, I think. Of course they do rather get them confused. If you watch for a little while, you can positively *see* the Muses hovering overhead, favoring first one and then another. Whoever wins is sure they've been working magnificently. Or if they've been working magnificently, they win; I'm not positive which.

Teddy says Gerry has won most often lately, while Charlie Baxter, as I might have guessed, usually loses. Gerry lost tonight, though; and no wonder, considering how Teddy discomfited him at dinner. As I told him – not very successfully. I should have remembered that Teddy Berg, who is known all over the world for his professional patience and generosity, in private life won't bear even the mildest criticism.

JANET: It wasn't very kind of you, quoting Gerry's poem back at him like that.
TEDDY: He deserved it. He was being ridiculous.
JANET: He only meant to be polite – not to shock Caroline.
TEDDY: My dear Janet. It would take a veryvery great deal more than that to shock Caroline. In her time, she has heard and seen things that would absolutely make us *blench*. It wasn't Caroline's ladylike sensibilities Gerry was protecting, m'dear. It was yours.

I met the two other guests who were sitting with Charlie and H. H. Waters at supper. The intellectual-looking man with the horn-rimmed glasses turns out to be a real intellectual: L. D. Zimmern, the critic. In spite of his reputation for difficulty, he's very pleasant – friendly, not at all dogmatic. He's up here finishing a new book on The Self in Contemporary American Literature.

The man in the red shirt who was talking and laughing so loudly is Nick Donato, a painter from New York. Not a painter, really; his things in the little gallery here are mostly hardware and neon tubing. Good-natured, but awfully crude – an odd type for Illyria, and he doesn't like Illyria much either, Teddy says. The history and tradition

of the place doesn't interest him, and he hates the décor.
You'd think he would at least appreciate the physical
amenities, but Teddy says not.

TEDDY: I don't think they mean a thing to him; he's probably longing for pizza.

JANET: Really? That's a pity.

TEDDY: Mm. Misses the city, doesn't like the cooking; and
he's always complaining that he lacks sexual release, I
understand ... In fact, m'dear, you'd better look out.
He'll probably be after you next.

Apparently Nick spent most of his first week here chasing
Sally Sachs (who's also a painter, but of a more traditional
sort), and almost catching her.

JANET: And what did happen to Sally, then?

TEDDY: Oh, she's going around with young Richard
Potter now. You saw him; they were sitting together at
dinner. It was all rather amusing. I'll tell you about it
sometime.

JANET: Tell me now.

TEDDY: Well. Poor Sally, when she arrived, week before
last – you know this is her first visit – I have no idea
what she expected to find at Illyria. But she certainly
wasn't prepared for the rush she got, probably for the
first time in her life ... Well, you saw her; you've got to
admit she's not madly attractive.

JANET: Rather interesting-looking, though, I thought.
Those big dark eyes –

TEDDY: Yes, she's a lot better now than I ever imagined
she could be. But when she first got here ... There's a
type of woman artist, not all of them by any means, but
some, you know, who seem to take up making pretty
pictures because they've despaired of painting their own
faces enough to make any difference. They may be full
of sexual energy, but they've given up on themselves as
objects. So they wear jeans three sizes too large and
scrub their faces raw and comb their hair straight down,

blah. That was our Sally ... Well, so-o-o, when she found herself at beauteous Illyria, being absolutely *pursued* night and day by a lot of good-looking men, she was flabbergasted. Leonard wasn't here yet, but all the rest of them (pointing) – Nick, Charlie, even Gerry was after her at first, though he claims now it's not so ... Of course they weren't seriously interested, they just wanted to amuse themselves. It was a competitive game, like croquet. Trying to see who could get his ball through the wicket first. But Nick was trying hardest.

JANET: And then Richard Potter arrived; is that the story?

TEDDY: No; he was here all along, actually. He was interested too, of course. But Ricky's shy. He didn't know how to buck the competition.

JANET: He looks like a nice boy.

TEDDY: Oh he is, very. And he's got possibilities as a musician, you know. A real melodic gift. He's written some interesting things already. Harmonically he's still rather tight; a bit theoretical, you know. Overcautious technically. It's his costive Middle Western WASP background – well, I needn't tell *you* about that. But it's always seemed to me that a passionate affair might do him a *lot* of good. Anyhow, I have great hopes for him now.

Whenever he speaks about music, Teddy's voice drops a full octave into seriousness. Even the tempo changes: *andante moderato*; suddenly he seems an impressive, mature person. A world-famous musician. Of course he is this person, to the world. So which is real? I suppose one would have to say, both. But it's not like the classic split personality, which doesn't know its other half. They co-exist – even collaborate: because of Theodore Berg's good opinion of Potter's talent, Teddy is slyly arranging his love life.

JANET: But what happened? ... *Something* must have

happened ... Do you mean that you – somehow you brought them together?

TEDDY: Oh, not that, hardly. The sex instinct, I think you'd have to call it, did that.

JANET: But you helped somehow.

TEDDY: Well, yes. I felt I had to do something. Professional loyalty, you know. We musicians have to stick together, we're in such a minority here.

JANET: So what did you do?

TEDDY: Nothing, really. I merely cleared away the debris a little. I simply mentioned to Sally, in casual conversation as it were, a few facts about some of her fellow guests I thought she ought to know. What a sweet devoted girl Gerry's wife is ... The amount of alimony Charlie has to pay ... Something of Nick's reputation in New York, and the responsibility he has, with a wife and five children –

JANET: *Five* children?

TEDDY: Five. Well, you know pop artists. They admire mass production ... And then I invited Sally and Richard over to my studio one evening to hear some tapes, and sent them off early together, and that was that.

Apart from his sympathy for another musician, one can see why Teddy (or anyone) might want to frustrate Nick Donato, who's so cheerfully aggressive. Though he'd never even heard of croquet before this summer, he's gone at it so hard that now he quite often wins – as he did tonight – and when he does, he completely ignores the rule that a victor must show decent modesty and reserve. Instead he shouts and grins and waves his croquet mallet, demands applause from the spectators. And not merely applause. I can see just how he must have behaved with Sally Sachs, from the offhand, rather arrogant way in which he immediately asked me out.

NICK: Hey, Janet. You want to come to the flicks tonight?

JANET: What? Oh, I don't think so, thank you.

NICK: Aw, come on. They're showing –
JANET: I'm afraid I can't. I promised Teddy I'd go and hear him play.

My first lie at Illyria, and quite unnecessary: I should have simply said I wanted to work. I didn't think of it, I suppose because I didn't want to work. So that would have been a lie too, though a less embarrassing one ... I was saved some embarrassment anyhow, because Teddy, only raising his eyebrows very slightly, went along with my lie, and even turned it into a truth.

JANET: I'm sorry I used you as an excuse like that, but I –
TEDDY: Oh, not at all. I quite understand. (Giggles) As a matter of fact, why don't you drop over to the studio a little later? I'm not going to play, but I'll give you a drink. Harmonia's coming too. About ten, say?

So the best part of the day was the last. Though I was very uncomfortable at first; more awkward and awed by Miss Waters (I can't call her Harmonia, as Teddy does) than I've been by anyone in years. At home, whatever happens or whomever I meet, a part of me always remains detached and even amused, observing it all. No matter how I feel, somewhere up in the back of my mind is the writer taking notes, remembering dialogue. (As Philip Roth is reported to have said once, 'We're lucky: nothing truly bad can happen to us. It's all material.') Even here, and even with someone as famous – though in another field – as Teddy Berg, I still have that sensation. But H. H. Waters is three times as much 'the writer' as I. Meeting her, I felt fearfully vulnerable.

Not that she acts, or looks, at all frightening. I knew from photographs that she wasn't and never could have been either beautiful or stylish. In fact, she's so plain as to be nearly grotesque, with long-lashed bulging eyes, buckteeth, a receding chin. Wisps of hair like gray hay falling from the stack on top of her head, and twiglike bits of hairpins sticking out of it. It doesn't seem fair or just – certainly not Poetic Justice – that the author of *Imaginary Gardens* should look like that. The only appropriate thing is her voice: low and musical, with a soft Southern accent.

We were awfully stiff at first. I tried clumsily to express my pleasure at meeting her, my long (deep, wide, high) admiration of her poems. She replied in polite Southern monosyllables. Janet, this is ridiculous, I told myself. Forty-two years old, the mother of two huge children, author of sixteen and a half published stories, and you're afraid of an elderly woman with no chin? Admittedly, she is a famous poet, but what harm can come to you from that? Besides, she's probably feeling as awkward as you are.

As soon as I had thought that, I realized it was more than true. What I was partly suffering from was HHW's own contagious shyness. And I remembered that she's famous for this; she is almost a recluse, seldom comes to New York. I felt better, but still didn't know what to say. Neither did she. We smiled at each other with nervous good will.

Luckily, at this point Teddy came back with our drinks (tea with brandy for Miss Waters) and began to entertain us. He has a great store of tales about this place – some perhaps apocryphal. Tonight he told some wonderful ghost stories. He says Jimmie, Paula's old dog, has been heard howling behind the garage on cold nights (she died there last Christmas); and that a distracted, dishonored Woman in White sometimes appears in the woods out behind the farthest studios. Wind and snow would explain both these apparitions, which have a nice Illyrian tone.

Less credibly, Teddy claims that Undine Moffat herself haunts his bedroom, which used to be hers. Her tasseled and canopied bed is still there, her rosewood desk inlaid with mother-of-pearl, her portrait in pink and white gauze draperies, and a gold-framed photostat of her last letter to the Illyria Foundation:

... As I envision the years to come, I look down again upon my beloved Illyria, upon the beauteous gardens and shady forests, bosky dells and crystal lakes, which have been so dear to my heart and lent such inspiration to my own poems. And lo, there I see them all – poets, painters, musicians, dramatists, essayists – creating, creating, creating ...

But somehow it's not the right setting for a spirit, all that turn-of-the-century opulence: gilt mirrors, salmon-pink satin and plush. And Undine, who according to report weighed nearly two hundred pounds by the time she died, would make rather a comic ghost.

Idea for story: The plump ghost. Seen by woman who is dieting. Unsuccessfully? When she succeeds (fails?), it vanishes. Her past or future self.

Teddy's only fault as a storyteller is a tendency to the silly-suggestive, regardless of his audience. When he remarked that the Woman in White is said to have been seduced in a toolshed by one of the Moffats' Italian gardeners, Miss Waters smiled, but her smile was pale, like skim milk.

Teddy's ghosts cured our fright, all the same, and we began to talk. Miss Waters' manner remained very diffident; she made the most unusual, original observations in the mildest, flattest way possible. We discussed writers versus artists versus musicians – a favorite Illyria topic. Painting and music as the two opposing arts (they can never meet unless united by words, as in opera; or gestures, as in ballet). One presumes you can't hear, the other that you can't see. You are supposed to be able to look at pictures in a gallery when they're tearing up the street outside – or listen to a concert without being distracted by the sight of a lot of not particularly attractive men in evening clothes sitting in chairs on a raised platform, restlessly and continually moving their arms back and forth. Fans, and even more practitioners, of these arts must develop a protective blindness or deafness. This would explain why musicians so often dress badly (Teddy's shabby tan sweater and pale-blue skewed bow tie), and painters have rather muted, colorless voices. And why, even at Illyria, most of us have no idea what the rest are doing.

All the same, we believe in each other's work; we know that's why we're all here, in this small private Eden. That *is* what it's like, Teddy and Miss Waters agreed.

This Eden isn't designed for human beings, though. Instead, we're all, temporarily, gods – busy creating. Of course, as Miss Waters said, we like to think of ourselves as creating innocently, without responsibility, for we only create ghosts – though sometimes rather plump ghosts.

June 30

I've begun to work again — wrote three pages of the plump-ghost story. It's so much easier here; so peaceful, not only physically but psychologically; even politically. The fretful trivia of domestic life, and the outer world of telegrams and anger, have receded to insignificance down a long avenue of pine trees, beyond the iron gates of the estate. There's no radio in the Mansion except in the servants' wing, no television. The newspapers are laid out every morning on the hall table; but we discuss the bad news of the day as if it were already history.

It's unfair, really, that I can come to Illyria every year merely because I write stories, and my friends who don't can't — though they need it just as much. No — more. Because by the time one's invited here, one has already constructed a sort of Illyria inside one's head.

There ought to be an Illyria Foundation for housewives. Some place just as beautiful and unworldly as this, with the same facilities — library, gardens, pool, lakes and woods; wonderful food and no responsibilities — where they could walk and read and rest and talk. The foundation could pay for housekeepers for those who have young children at home and no full-time help, like Peggy and Jennifer — they need it most of all. (Of course, not everyone could profit from this sort of vacation, or would even appreciate it; there would have to be a selection committee.)

Interesting conversation at breakfast with Charlie Baxter and Leonard Zimmern, about the general effect of Illyria on guests. Leonard says it makes him feel (and write) as if he were in a James novel, staying at one of those great country houses – Gardencourt or Fawns.

LEONARD: I don't know if it's objective, but I often get the sense lately that I'm making terribly subtle distinctions, uncovering the hidden meaning of some line –

CHARLIE: You 'get the sense'?

LEONARD: What? Oh; exactly. You see, it seems quite natural to speak that way, here.

But what matters (as in James?) isn't so much the style of life at Illyria, but its pace – the feeling of having all the time in the world to make such distinctions; being relieved of all one's petty everyday responsibilities. 'Being guests, instead of hosts,' as Charlie said.

I realize who Charlie is now. (I thought he looked familiar yesterday, but decided he was only a familiar type.) He's C. Ryan Baxter, who wrote *The Red Moon,* that experimental novel about the American Revolution (with Marxist overtones) that won so many prizes just after the war. I suppose I thought, if I thought anything, that he must be dead. Instead he's here at Illyria, hiding from his ex-wife and other creditors. Leonard told me later, after the others had left, what's happened to him since 1950.

LEONARD: A couple of flops – trouble with the Senate Investigating Committee, compounded by the fact that Baxter's probably the most thickheadedly sincere political innocent who ever held a card, if he ever *did* hold a card. Writer's block ... A bad drinking problem ... A ruinous divorce, which left him owing more alimony per year than he can make in five now; but his wife was a stupid beautiful girl who convinced herself and the judge that Charlie had stopped writing best sellers deliberately in order to impoverish her, and could start again any time he wanted to ...

After that? Well, he's had jobs in little colleges ... A

few stories and poems in little magazines. He got a couple of grants, but that was a while ago – foundations prefer writers on their way up.

Now he's on the wagon again, at least. He has this job here, free room and board for three months and a chance to pay off some of his debts – maybe finish the novel he's been working on for the last five years.

JANET: Do you think he will?

LEONARD: I don't know. I certainly hope so.

And so do I. Considering what he's been through, Charlie's amazingly unembittered; gentle, often wryly charming.

I like Leonard too, though usually I distrust critics. He does tend a bit to *criticize*, to point out faults. (When I remarked that Illyria was like Eden, he said, 'Yes, and with the same Do Not Touch notices on everything.') But at least he doesn't, like most critics, seem to view writers as a necessary evil: undependable artisans gifted with strength and skill but not much intelligence or taste – ignorant cottage workers, really, whose products must be refined and packaged to be fit for public consumption.

CHARLIE: Don't underrate the materialistic side of this place, Janet. If your standard of living's sort of sub-standard ... When you're used to making yourself instant coffee and cornflakes for breakfast, for instance, in a Greenwich Village kitchenette; all this space and luxury –

JANET: But it's not only that; it's the whole atmosphere. None of us is used to this style of life.

LEONARD: But we should be. What you've all got to remember is that this is what you deserve.

This of course pleased us both: I stopped feeling guilty about my comparatively comfortable life in Westford; Charlie began to talk about Eastern Europe, where 'they order these things better.'

We were interrupted by the arrival of Nick Donato, who was less interested in conversation than in eating as much breakfast as possible as rapidly as possible; mopping up his plate with slices of toast and licking fried egg off his fingers afterward.

The trouble is, Illyria is such a perfect place that one wants everyone here (including oneself, of course) to be perfectly worthy of it. Whereas anyone makes mistakes now and then – even selection committees. As I said to Leonard afterward.

JANET: I've often thought, if Undine Moffat could see some of the people she's, so to speak, invited here, she'd be most surprised. She'd probably say, 'Stop pretending to be an artist and leave my house, you rude, vulgar person.'

LEONARD: Oh, I don't know. I think more likely she would just overlook it, in the grand style ... Besides, you know, Nick was probably *taught* to wipe his plate like that, as a child in the slums, when food was scarce.

He meant to rebuke me, though mildly. And I suppose he was right. Nick certainly behaved unaesthetically, but I shouldn't have remarked on it. And he has more excuse than I do: as a child, I learned better manners.

I suppose I was irritated by Nick because he interrupted a conversation about my book, which Leonard turns out to have read. And even more because of the way he did it.

NICK: You a writer? Hey, Baxter, pass the salt. Yeah, I thought you looked like a lady writer.

That looks harmless written down, but it wasn't; it was coarse and dismissive.

Of course, it's been said before, though not in that tone of voice. What's occasionally meant (and sometimes also said) is that I look a little like pictures of Virginia Woolf – a less fine drawn, less neurasthenic, middle-class American version. (Pictures of me, on the other hand, seldom catch any such resemblance, perhaps because the camera adds another ten pounds to the ten I must already have on her.) Somebody asked once if that was why I decided to become a writer. 'Not at all,' I replied indignantly. 'Long before I even *heard* of VW, I wanted to be a writer.' Quite true, but so do a lot of young girls. And who can say it didn't influence me when I found out? Standing in the library stacks at Smith, with Daiches' biography open in my hand, feeling a deep sentimental shock of recognition . . .

When people in Westford say I look like a writer, though, my first reaction is to check my stockings for runs, my hands for ink – because that's what they usually mean. The've seen, or imagined they've seen, some flaw in my disguise as the conservatively attractive, well-dressed wife of an insurance executive. Which isn't a disguise anyhow, but half of the truth.

A lady writer. And why should I mind that, anyway? Do I mind being a writer? Or being a lady?

Later

A perfect summer day. I finished two pages; went to the pool for lunch and a swim; came back, and did two pages more.

Kenneth's here already – he just arrived. It's wonderfully good to see him again.

There was an odd moment when he came into the room and for a second I didn't recognize him. I hadn't expected him until later; that was partly it. Also, perhaps, I was surprised that he should have to arrive at all; I really believe he's always at Illyria.

Anyhow, there was a knock on the door, I said 'Come in,' and a man in his early fifties, fair-skinned, gray-haired, of medium height or a little less, of average weight or a little more, came in. He looked tired. I had time to notice all this; then he said 'Janet?' and I saw it was Kenneth.

What I really think is that the man who came in wasn't the real (my, the Illyria) Kenneth Foster, *because* he had only just arrived, and still had the dust of the outside world on him (figurative dust—he'd already washed and changed). His face was stiff and inexpressive, and he moved differently, without that characteristic springy step. And though he was early, he'd had a long hard trip.

KENNETH: Roz stripped the gears on my bus yesterday, and she couldn't drive me up herself, so I had to take the small car. If you've ever tried to fit a month's painting equipment into a Mustang convertible ...

JANET: Oh, dear. You have a Mustang now?

KENNETH: Roz bought it last month. Also the gas gauge is set wrong – Roz knew it, but of course she never did anything about it, so I ran out of gas on the turnpike. I had to walk about two miles.

JANET: That's awful. Are you very tired?

KENNETH: No. Just a bit.

JANET: For goodness' sake, sit down, then.

Once he'd sat down and had some iced tea, Kenneth began to look more like himself. But it took time. I kept scanning his face while we talked, as if it were a strange landscape. A scene agreeable rather than picturesque – Mid-western rather than Alpine. Smooth rolling plains, only slightly eroded with age; regular features of moderate dimensions, given an air of intellectuality by the recession of vegetation on the upper slopes. (SAVE THIS)

JANET: I'm sorry I haven't anything stronger than tea. I could go and borrow some gin from Teddy Berg, if you like –

KENNETH: Please don't bother. Really. It's a pleasure for me, you know, not to have to think about alcohol at this time of day. Just sit down, Janet, and tell me all the news.

Slowly, as in a Wordsworth poem, the landscape became personified. It was, one realized, full of lively interest, originality and charm – of an unobtrusive but generous sympathy.

Especially good to be able to talk to him about my work again. I suppose all writers have their ideal imaginary reader: a vaguely outlined godlike person who smiles at all their jokes, picks up every reference; remembers and understands everything. One never really expects to meet him. Only I did, after twenty years – Kenneth is my ideal reader.

JANET: It's better already since I've been here. I knew it would be. You know I've been really quite depressed – I wrote you – these last few months.

KENNETH: I remember you said something about that. But at the same time you sent me copies of two impressively good stories.

JANET: But they were so short. Hardly stories at all.

KENNETH: What has length to do with it? That's like telling me a picture by Rubens is ten times better than one by Vermeer, because it's ten times larger.

JANET: Did you like them, really? The one about the amateur astronomer, I thought it was rather slight, rather ...

KENNETH: It was a beautiful story.

JANET: I know you said so, but – I don't know how to put it ... Perhaps it's not that there's so much wrong with the stories themselves; maybe I've just got tired of writing them. Describing things – inventing dialogue, and finding the right word. Making little gray marks on paper. You know.

KENNETH: Of course I know. Everyone goes through these periods.

JANET: It's so awful while it lasts, though. Awful. Every story I've written or thought of writing for months, as

soon as I look at it again, it begins to remind me of
something I've already done, or else read somewhere. I
don't know. Maybe I ought to try something new,
more experimental ... Different forms ... Different
subjects, maybe –

KENNETH: You're completely wrong. Excuse me, Janet,
but I couldn't bear it if you let yourself be influenced
by this frantic search for something new, some grotesque idea or technique, that's going on everywhere now.

He understands because he has the same problems, only
worse. The anxiety I've felt this spring about being
repetitious or 'outdated' is part of a general epidemic.

KENNETH: There are people now composing sonatas
that consist of turning a couple of portable radios off
and on, and writing novels where you're supposed to
shuffle the pages at random. Only most musicians and
writers don't take them seriously, so far ... Half the
students I get today – no, more than half this year –
are infected by it. They think they can become famous
artists overnight, if they can only invent some new
gimmick.

It's not their fault, really, they're just following the
crowd. Art's become a kind of magic Bingo. A get-rich-
quick scheme for a few unscrupulous dealers and
critics in New York and their protégés ... I'm not talking about the few serious artists who've legitimately
worked their way through to new styles. It's all these
Dead End kids who've never learned to draw or handle
paint.

Some of Kenneth's most promising students have quit his
classes for those of a visiting pop artist named Bill Eats,
and are now gluing angora fur on radiators and making
pornographic collages twelve feet long out of the local
telephone directory. And even the ones who remain have
becomes impossible.

KENNETH: I had a girl in my life class this spring,

instead of drawing the model, she stuck a lot of old paint rags onto her canvas and poured a can of varnish over them. 'What's that supposed to be?' I asked her. 'I feel the possibilities of the picture plane have been exhausted,' she told me.

I couldn't help laughing at this, and at Kenneth's imitation of his student's manner, but he wouldn't laugh. 'No, no,' he said in a bleak voice. 'It's gone too far for comedy.' And I looked at him and seemed to see the survivor of some disaster sitting on my sofa as if it were a cot in a first-aid station; half-stunned, disoriented.

But Kenneth's disaster wasn't at the University, or in New York, really; it was much nearer home. I thought it might be that, but couldn't tell if he wanted to talk about it; he almost never has.

JANET: Roz wasn't able to drive you up today?

KENNETH: You could put it that way.

JANET: You mean she didn't want to?

KENNETH: I didn't ask her. Roz got in last night, this morning, rather, at about three AM, and she was in no condition to drive a car. So I didn't bother to wake her . . . She passed out in the living room.

JANET: You left her a note?

KENNETH: She knows where I am.

But it's not only that Roz drinks too much, which I already knew.

JANET: Has she been worse then, lately?

KENNETH: No. About the same really. The only change is that her . . . drinking companions keep getting younger.

JANET: Getting . . . younger?

KENNETH: Relatively, at least, if not absolutely. The current one is about thirty-five, I believe.

JANET: Oh, Kenneth . . . You mean, it's serious?

KENNETH: That depends on your point of view. Roz doesn't take it seriously. As she's told me more than once, all she wants is to have a good time. And I suppose some people would say she's justified ... No. You see, emotional attachments don't interest Roz. As far as she's concerned, they don't exist. She just needs a little fun, as she puts it.

And so she sleeps around. 'Has love affairs' would be a nicer way of putting it, but not accurate. They're not affairs, and don't involve love. Just casual incidents. An architect whose wife is away – an old acquaintance passing through town on business ...

I remember now that two years ago when Roz came to drive him home, Kenneth apologized for not inviting me out to lunch along with Curt and Hortense – saying that if I were called to his wife's attention, she would never believe that our friendship was platonic, because such friendships were outside her experience.

What seems strange is that all these people, some of them much younger, would *want* to sleep with Roz, who's fifty at least, overweight and no beauty, though she does have a kind of raddled prettiness. I suppose that's naïve; probably there are lots of men who could fall into bed with anything that looked like a woman, after a night's hard drinking. But also I don't understand how Roz could want to do something so sordid and meaningless – and painful to Kenneth, whatever he says:

KENNETH: It doesn't disturb me so much any more, you know. It only seems pathetic. It's Roz's way of staying young. Her grasp at immortality.

Really, Kenneth and I are incredibly lucky – all of us here are – not having even to think of grabbing at immortality in that miserable way.

Knowing about Roz explains a lot – so much that I probably should have guessed it before. But until now, whenever Kenneth's spoken of her, or I of Clark, we've only complained about the sort of things that can be complained about lightly and humorously. And so I (stupidly) assumed that, like me, he had nothing worse to complain of.

I understand better now what I've sometimes thought of as Kenneth's odd lack of sympathy with people's love affairs (when he's so sympathetic about their other concerns), his tendency to rather downgrade that side of things. As when I told him about Sally Sachs and Ricky Potter earlier.

JANET: ... so you see, Teddy was really responsible for bringing them together.

KENNETH: Or so he imagines. Teddy's always thinking he sees sexual intrigues, when in fact it's one of the best things about Illyria that there's so little of that here. Most people are too busy working to bother. You know – it's like when you meet Caroline or Paula at dinner. They don't say 'How are you today?' Instead they ask 'How is your work going?' And that seems quite natural. The assumption is that you have no private life, at least while you're at Illyria.

It was an awful conversation, about Roz. I wanted to *know* everything (I always do, really), but at the same time I didn't want to *hear* it. We were both very strained, though we pretended to be casual. When the subject changed, there was terrific relief; I felt as if Kenneth and I had just got safely through a dark railway tunnel, where at any moment something hugely awkward might come rushing at us; or I might have made a misstep, an error in tact or tone, which would have hurt our friendship permanently. And I think he felt the same.

But since it was there, we had to go through the tunnel, I see that, to get to the sunny country on the other side – to get to Illyria.

Late

A fine evening. Worked a bit after supper, and then about nine went out to a place over in Jerico called

Lola's, a rural bohemian hangout, all of us more or less got up as rural bohemians. It began at supper when Teddy said as a joke that Lola wouldn't admit Leonard in his professor costume. L. said, very well, he'd change and dress the part. And so then we all did. Everyone went, even H. H. Waters, who hadn't changed but somehow looked right in her fading sweater and falling hair. Kenneth and I were all in black; Leonard had a magnificent pop-art tie borrowed from Nick D., and Gerry outdid himself in a flowered shirt and beads. Teddy, with a bandanna knotted around his neck, looked like a fat old pirate. We drank espresso and beer, and danced to the jukebox.

I've always thought I shared Clark's dislike of masquerade parties. The ones at home are invariably (beneath the noise and bustle) sad and silly. In spite of the elaborate costumes, the expensive rented wigs and satins and spangles, the sheets draped with careful facetiousness into Roman folds, no one looks or feels any different. But the people tonight weren't 'wearing costumes' in that sense – they *were* rural bohemians, for the moment.

They all looked very good; better than people in Westford do. Not that they're more handsome – by conventional standards most of them are less handsome; it's something else, something in their manner. Maybe it's because they were really at a party, and not a disguised meeting of the League of Women Voters, the Friends of the Library, the Hospital Auxiliary, the Chamber of Commerce, the local Republican and Democratic clubs, and the Westford Casualty Company – which is what most of our parties actually are.

'So why do you bother with them?' asked Teddy Berg, to whom I was telling all this. 'You should leave those dreary people and come to New York.'

Of course I couldn't do that; and even if I could, I wouldn't, though I didn't say so to Teddy. A few days in New York are fun; more would be exhausting. It's not another, larger Illyria, but the opposite. Ugly, tense, dangerous; full of rubbish and noise; of cultural middlemen and hangers-on. I've never been to a New York party where the real artists weren't outnumbered by reviewers, editors, publishers, collectors, dealers and agents. Plus, of course, everybody's wives and mistresses, and all those unattached or semi-attached girls referred to by Kenneth's friends as 'chicks.' (It's one of the best things about Illyria that there are no chicks here.)

In the city, as Paula said, most people look angry and unhappy. They look older than they should, too – older than they really are. Again the opposite of Illyria, which as Kenneth says is a sort of Shangri-la. Everyone who comes here seems to lose ten years; and if you live here permanently the effect is even greater. Caroline Kent is well over seventy, and she looks about fifty-five; Paula looks forty.

But what's even more important is that age doesn't matter here. All the labels by which people outside separate themselves into tight little groups – Age, Sex, Class, Race, Religion – have been left off. Even success and failure don't count: if you're here, you *are* a success.

It's remarkable really what diverse and naturally antagonistic types have lived together at Illyria for weeks and months as peaceably as the animals in an Edward Hicks painting: Norman Podhoretz and Ned Rorem; James Baldwin and Louise Bogan. Interesting too that Caroline has avoided publicity so successfully that one never reads or hears of the place. There is an odd mist over it, which one not only feels but sooner or later learns to exude. One wouldn't deny having been here if one were asked, but otherwise one just doesn't mention it to outsiders.

But is this all Caroline's doing, or is it that being an artist is like being in a sort of secret society anyhow? Perhaps that's why I already feel that all the people here are my friends, or potential friends. Very different from Westford, where it takes years really to make friends – and even then they're mostly friends in the plural sense:

friends of the Family. I don't know them the way I know Kenneth.

It's so good, seeing him again. There's nothing we can't say to each other, and so wonderfully much we don't have to say. No need to explain and define everything the way one usually must.

It's after twelve. (We stayed out late, for Illyria, because we were having such a good time.) A warm, windy night. Down below the rose garden I can hear cars whirring past on the thruway, or/like gusts of wind. Gusts of wind like cars whirring past? (SAVE THIS)

Very happy. I think it's going to be my best visit yet.

July 1

Another cloudless summer day. The *Times* predicts New York temperatures over 100; here it's warm but pleasant, with light winds lifting and shredding the heat. Ideal Illyria weather – though the gardeners, Caroline says, want rain.

Finished a first draft of the ghost story this morning. It's too short, only nine pages, but I think not bad. I've done in two days what would have taken weeks at home. And besides that, I feel calmer, happier, nicer – most of all, *normal*. Though I'm here because I'm a writer, paradoxically it's only here that I don't have to be 'a writer.' I can be an ordinary person again, not what I've been in Westford for the last six months: a sort of dangerous freak.

I used to think in my girlish naïveté that it would be wonderful to become an author. It didn't occur to me that if this happened I would, in the eyes of most people, partly cease to be a human being. No one had ever told me about the worst industrial hazard of literature – the poisonous gas of reputation which is discharged around every writer in direct proportion to his success.

I don't mean just that one is in danger of breathing in this gas oneself and swelling up with vanity or self-consciousness, which sooner or later ruins one's work. Even if he is personally immune, his work suffers because his anonymity as an observer has been destroyed. People around him breathe the gas, and their behavior is distorted in his presence, just as it would be in front of a camera. A really famous writer, for instance, must seldom meet anybody who isn't consciously in the unnatural situation of meeting a famous writer.

Since *At Home* was only a moderate success, I suffered from poison gas only moderately. Soon after the book came out I began to notice something Philip Roth was talking about last year: the peculiar manner of most people when meeting a writer for the first time. Some are cool, suspicious and formal; they know already they won't like you, because they don't like writers. Others gush and grow artificially warm. They act like interesting subjects or make sensitive and perceptive remarks which they have prepared beforehand. They call one's attention to poetic aspects of nature ('Did you notice those fuzzy yellow flowers on the birch tree outside, just like little ...'), and propose some quaint metaphor, in the hope of seeing it appear eventually in one's work. (I recognize the process instantly, because I used to do the same thing myself.) Others prefer to describe the Unforgettable Characters they have met, or insist on telling some anecdote which they would immortalize If Only They Could Write Like You.

But the reactions of strangers, however uncomfortable, are unimportant. It was my friends who hurt, even my best friends; beginning to look at me oddly as they smelled the gas, then drawing away a little. They had found out something they had always known but hadn't taken any account of – that I was a 'writer.' That is, I was not like them, but different in a peculiar and not really very attractive way. So they didn't see me as often as before; and when they did, they made jokes about how if they told me something I would put it, or them, into one of my stories. Or worse, suspected me of having done so already, and took bitter offense, like Julia Martin.

JULIA: I read your story in the *Atlantic*. That woman who screams at her children, that's me, isn't it?
JANET: No, of course not!

JULIA: Well, George and everyone else thinks it is. If it's not supposed to be me, why did you call her Julia? I must say, I thought that wasn't very nice.

And though I tried vehemently to explain that if I'd meant that character for her (or even thought of her at all), I wouldn't have used her name, Julia wasn't really convinced. 'Yes, I suppose so,' she said, and pretended to be satisfied. But I could see she wasn't, and that our friendship was over. And even this wasn't the worst. The worst effect of *At Home* was right at home. It was as if a delayed bomb had gone off in our house, hissing poisonous smoke, and Clark and the children, looking around, coughing and weeping, saw me holding the fuse.

Clark doesn't believe me, but I really had no idea it was loaded. I remember the day Candida told me that the publishers wanted to make the book longer and include some of my early writing. My only reaction was innocent pleasure that now these stories would be saved from their burial alive in the dark basement stacks of libraries – they would be brought into the light again, so everyone would see them.

And so everyone did, including Clark's mother, who wrote at once to ask us if Clary still took things from stores, like the little girl in 'Happy Easter'; and Miss Lily Raik, Clark's former secretary, whom we used to call 'The Artificial Flower.' And that awful man at the theater benefit party in New York who kept kidding Clark because he knows nothing of the insides of cars and is always being made a fool of by garage mechanics, as revealed by me years ago in 'See America First.'

And the boy at Clarkie's school who began spreading it around that Stockwell's mother had written a dirty story called 'Paying Guests.' At first I couldn't think what he meant. But then I reread the story, and realized it must be because of the scene where Maura is watching the caretaker's little boy sliding in the bathtub after the water has run out. It's a big old-fashioned tub with iron claw feet, which he tells her is alive and walks around the farm-house at night. And other similar stories, which she (being a year or two older) doesn't really believe; and so when he tells her the facts of life, she doesn't believe them either.

When I wrote that story, I didn't even think of the possible social effects it might have. Clark's position in the company and the magazines I appeared in were both relatively obscure. We lived a mildly unconventional private life then: entertained mostly our old friends from college; drove down often to graduate-student parties in New Haven, returning past midnight to make cinnamon toast in the kitchen after the sitter had gone home, or love on the living-room rug. The house was smaller and not in such good condition, but it belonged to us. It wasn't always full of other people: live-in help and teen-agers and committee members and people who work with or for Clark, and their dreary wives.

Nowadays, especially since the book came out, everything is different. I have to think that if the story I'm working on turns out to be successful (i.e., is accepted by the *Atlantic, Harper's*, or *The New Yorker*), every word I write is going to be read by most of these people; by Clark Jr and Clarissa; by Clark's parents, and his brother Bobby, and his sister Emmy, and Emmy's stuffy husband. And their friends.

I suppose it's no wonder I haven't been able to work very well lately. Or can only write sketches.

If I were writing 'Paying Guests' now, I would be more careful. I would take out a sentence or two here and there, or put them differently; indicate everything more subtly. The story would be shorter then, slighter ... But does that mean it would be less good? Kenneth would say, of course not.

At breakfast Teddy told us that Caroline's goddaughter, Anna May, has finally (implying, after much equivocation) agreed to come up for the benefit concert this weekend. She's arriving tonight. Odd to think that Illyria seems uninteresting, even boring, to anyone – but I suppose it would to a young girl impatient for experience of the 'real world.' (Apparently Anna May's not particularly artistic or literary.) A duty visit to an elderly lady in the remote country; something she goes through every year, but probably more and more unwillingly, pushed from behind by her parents. (She is Caroline's heir, and – according to Teddy – Caroline's quite well off.)

TEDDY: You can imagine – living here absolutely free for forty years, with a very generous salary. And she has something of her own besides. Not to mention what must be by now a really fabulous collection of letters, all the paintings and drawings people have given her ...

Local reaction to the news was surprising. Charlie and Teddy, who already know Anna May, were tolerant:

CHARLIE: I haven't seen her since she was thirteen. She was an awfully pretty child then. Very self-possessed. Of course now she must be nineteen, twenty ...

But everyone else was either aggressively uninterested or quite hostile. They asked whether Caroline often invited her relatives up for free vacations, said they hoped she wouldn't expect them to be social, etc.

Teddy says, though, that nobody's likely to see much of Anna May even if they want to; Caroline won't allow it.

TEDDY: And if you know which side your toast is buttered on, you'll all leave Anna May strictly a-lone. You won't get much of a chance at her anyhow, if this is like the last summer she was up here.

It was very funny really. Ed Loomis was here then, and Jonathan Baumbach. They practically fell off their chairs when she walked into the dining room, in a little pink dress with ruffles here and here. She must have been about sixteen then. Before we got to dessert, it'd somehow gone around the room that anyone caught seducing Anna May, or even trying to, would be thrown right out of Illyria on his little behind. Just to make sure, Caroline pretty well never let her out of her sight ... Every morning, Anna May used to lie out in a deck chair in front of Caroline's house, toasting herself in the sun, in a wee tiny white bikini. All the fellows routed their morning walk in that direction, but they didn't dare come too close. It was a veryvery tense weekend, though, especially in the evenings.

Since then, Anna May hasn't been up for the summer season. She visits Caroline in the wintertime, when there's just a few guests around – old friends of the family like Harmonia and me.

After lunch

Had a marvelous swim and lunch with Kenneth at the pool. He'd slept late and was looking much better. He was amused when I told him about Caroline's goddaughter's visit and everyone's reaction to it. But not surprised – says he feels the same himself. That, after all, Illyria is a place where men come to get away from women. And he enumerated: Gerry and Nick are escaping from houses full of children and diapers, Ricky from an interfering mother, Charlie from the ex-wife whose alimony he can't pay, and Leonard from his students at Sarah Lawrence and a demanding girl friend. And (he didn't say and didn't need to) himself from Roz. So the idea that women are invading Illyria exasperates them all.

'But what about H. H. Waters and Sally Sachs and me?' I asked. 'We're women.'

'Oh, you don't count,' he replied. 'You're on our side.'

I'm going to type the first draft of my story now, then reward myself by reading Jim McConkey's new book. I've also taken *Red Moon* and Gerry's latest collection of poems out of the library, will try to finish them while I'm here –

Why 'will try,' as if these books were a task, Jim's a

'reward'? I like Charlie and Gerry, I admire their work, but there *is* a reluctance – toward the form, I think; even the physical form – one book being too large for comfort, the other too small. Picking up a four-hundred-page novel like Charlie's requires actual muscular exertion. Its size implies that there is a leaden weight and duration to existence, that life contains very many persons and scenes, relationships of dense complexity. While Gerry's 'slim volume of verse,' with its spine bulging out beyond the covers in profile like a thin person with a huge head, is just the opposite. It suggests that experiences are extremely brief, lyric and limited – that we live solipsistically among blank white wastes of unconsciousness. One prefers something in between.

Besides, nowadays most long novels are bad. It was different a hundred or two hundred years ago. Today life moves faster, its parts are less connected; one assumes of most interesting events and relations (however intense) that they will be of no greater length or complication than can be described in twenty or thirty pages. So we choose the literary forms which match our lives. Or is it vice versa? When we write shorter and shorter stories, are we persuading our readers to divide their lives into ever smaller, bright, discontinuous bits?

After supper

I may have commended Illyria too soon on being free of chicks. Anna May Mundy looks like a chick if ever I saw one. I don't mean just that she's a very pretty young girl. Chicks are the special sort of pretty young girls who are romantically infatuated with art and artists. Usually without personal ambition, they're willing figuratively and literally to lie down at the feet of any fellow who's published a book or had a concert or a one-man show (good or mediocre – most have no critical sense). Victims of both the Feminine and the Artistic Mystique, they don't ask for ordinary courtesy or human consideration, invitations to dinner and the theater, or proposals of marriage. Though of course they do hope to become artists' wives, and a surprising number succeed. Ann Landers says men won't marry girls they don't respect; but artists and writers do. Some of them, indeed, do it over and over again, at about ten-year intervals – forgetting every time that chicks always turn into hens.

In the beginning, however, all a chick wants is the honor of sleeping with an artist, and if she's lucky getting her name into a poem, or her face and/or body on canvas – immortality again. The story about Robert Creeley: He was at a N.Y. party after a reading, and the host said to him, 'See that girl over there?' nodding across the room at a girl sitting on the sofa. 'She wants to make it with you tonight.' 'Well, uh, thanks very much,' Creeley said. 'Tell her I'm very honored and all that, but I'm married. I'm not interested in getting involved.' 'Oh, but she knows that,' his friend replied. 'All she wants is the *experience*.'

Besides, chicks disrupt the social structure. When I see too many of them at New York parties, I feel like an indignant Tory economist contemplating an influx of cheap foreign labor. With so many chicks available, men are going to decide (quite logically) that there's no reason to go to the trouble of meeting, courting, marrying and properly supporting non-chicks. Even those who don't take up with them are influenced unconsciously. They begin to treat their wives and mistresses like chicks; or else the wives and mistresses grow panicky and begin acting like chicks to meet the competition.

Of course, considered seriously, chicks are pathetic. Even if one were suffering from them personally, one would have to pity these immigrants. The sweatshop working conditions (cooking on a grimy hot plate in a dark corner of some studio, their few clothes hung on a pipe or crammed into a suitcase under his bed); the language barrier (at parties, no one speaks to a chick for long unless he's on the make); and worst of all, the lack of job security. Chicks are laid off early – sometimes as soon as their health or their looks begin to go; often left with two or three children to support on an inadequate or non-existent alimony, and no other marketable skills.

It's all the result of an unfortunate but common mistake : the mistake of thinking that artists aren't merely unlike other men when they're at work, but are different in some magical way at all times; whether they're drinking beer or riding on a bus or eating spaghetti or even sleeping (they have different and grander dreams, as one of Ken Noland's chicks once actually told me).

And one has to admit that Illyria might foster this error. As we left the dining room tonight we could see through the hall windows a little group of people, tourists, crossing the grass down by the fountain. (Under the Moffats' will, the formal gardens are open to the public several days a week from dawn till dusk, and this of course is the height of the season.) They paused and looked up the lawn toward us as if we were Rockefeller Center.

(Teddy says that when Daniel Lang was here last month, he was down by the rose garden one day eating lunch with a friend, and a family of tourists came through. A little boy saw them through the arbor, and he pointed his finger and cried out, 'Are those artists, Mom, or are they real people?')

And when one meets a girl like Anna May, destined from birth (or from christening, anyhow) to be become a chick, one can only feel pity. When one considers the deference she's seen shown to artists all her life – the leisured luxury in which they seem to live here, the gentle self-confidence of their manners – it would be only natural for her to think of them almost as gods.

But since we aren't gods, Anna May's awe is discomfiting. Her eager smiles and wide-eyed homage made Charlie, who sat next to her at dinner, look silly even from across the room. (The seating plan tonight was interesting. As usual when there are guests, Caroline asked certain people to her table – but this time instead of Teddy and

Miss Waters, she'd chosen those with the least reputation: Charlie and Richard Potter. Almost as if she wanted to spare the rest of us from distraction. Charlie certainly was distracted by Anna May – so much so that after dinner he forgot the croquet game and followed her back to Caroline's house to hear Teddy's new tapes.)

Anna May innocently made Charlie *look* silly; she made me *feel* silly. This from the moment we were introduced before dinner, when she (misunderstanding) repeated my name as 'Miss Belsmith.' I should have corrected her, but, discomfited, missed the right moment. (The foolish decision, when I first began to send out my stories in college, that plain 'Janet Smith' was too dull to interest any editor; that the addition of my rather silly middle name would make me seem more elegant, romantic, French – Now, of course, I can't get rid of it.)

And she made me look and feel old. Here at Illyria, where no one's under thirty, Sally Sachs seemed a *jeune fille*; and I was beginning to think of myself as an attractive young woman. Anna May's not strikingly beautiful, just a conventionally pretty college girl – but she's twenty. After dinner I came upstairs and looked in the glass; and there I saw a middle-aged person with a creased, rouged face, dingy graying curls, and too much make-up – Janet pretending to be Belle again.

Later

Feel considerably better. I conquered the impulse to hide in my room and went out to watch the croquet game, ended up playing – Gerry and I against Kenneth and Leonard. Then Kenneth, Gerry and I went over to the pool house for beer.

I've decided I like Gerry. I don't like his new book of poetry as well as the last – it's too strainedly spontaneous. And he does rather obviously believe in We and They (We who have dropped out of The System, They everyone else). Still, he has a touching quality. He's immensely serious about 'not selling out to Them,' and has kept to his resolve of two summers ago never to teach again. Absurd or not, it hasn't been easy. Gerry earns almost nothing from his writing: the advances on his two books (four years' work) only came to six hundred dollars, and most of the magazines he appears in pay little or nothing. He lives with his young wife and two very young children over the garage of a house on Long Island, where she does housework and cooking in exchange for their rent. They still owe money on a VW that's beginning to fall apart, and are in debt to several charitable friends. ('Of course,' Kenneth said later, 'he should never have married.')

Gerry's main income comes from foundation grants, often and anxiously applied for, and stretched to last as many years as possible; and from poetry readings. He makes from fifty to a hundred dollars a reading, depending on the size of his audience. After *Wet Dreams* appeared he 'got on the college circuit' – a New York agency contracted to send him around the country on tours whereby he can net seven hundred and fifty dollars in ten days. Which sounds good, until you learn what he has to do for it. Every day another city, another college (sometimes two); traveling all morning, met by some stranger at the airport or bus station; an official lunch, a seminar with writing students, a cocktail party and official dinner at the faculty club before his reading, an unofficial late drunken party afterward – all these not optional social events, but command *performances*. Long hours in queasy planes or grimy buses; short nights in motels, or on the lumpy sofa-bed of some acquaintance; institutional food and drink; and the same witless questions and spiteful criticisms repeated by students and professors with slightly different faces every twenty-four hours. I could never endure it.

And that's not even to mention what for me would be worst of all: having to stand up before crowds of strangers and read my work aloud. For Gerry, this isn't an infliction – he even enjoys it, being something of an actor. In fact, his size, his golden looks, his resonant voice, are at least as important professionally as his ability to arrange words. More important economically, since he usually reads other people's poems as well as his own. There ought to be a new name for Gerry's occupation; he's not a 'poet' in the sense that Dick Wilbur and Jimmy Merrill are; he's more a sort of medieval bard brought up to date.

One might think that in the end it would be less strain for him to take a teaching job, such as Kenneth has. But it's easier to be an artist at a university than to be a writer, as Kenneth himself pointed out; less oppressive.

KENNETH: College campuses are crowded with tired words – not so much with tired images. Also, painters and sculptors aren't harassed and outnumbered by their critics, the way a writer is in most English departments. They aren't made to lecture to survey courses, proctor exams, correct papers and read theses. I only have to teach painting.

I'm extremely lucky not to have to support myself (assuming I could, which is debatable) by giving readings, applying for grants, teaching 'creative writing' – or even just by writing. Trying to live on three or four thousand a year, which is about what I make on an average after Candida's fees and taxes ...

GERRY: The thing is, Janet, what you have is a patron, like in the eighteenth century.

That's amusing, and of course my book *is* dedicated to Clark – but it's not right. Clark doesn't support me because of my writing, but in spite of it. What I really have is a good job as a live-in housekeeper and companion to an executive. Reasonable salary, pleasant working conditions, permanent tenure, fringe benefits – although the hours are long, and after twenty years I only get two or three weeks' vacation every summer.

I'm also lucky to be an avant-garde writer. Ordinary life provides me with the material I need — I don't have to go out of my way to seek new experiences, new sensations. Whereas Gerry feels obligated to expand his consciousness in every available direction. He described to us two LSD trips he's been on, and it was obvious they were business trips; not taken for 'kicks' as a tourist or pleasure seeker, but because he thought it his professional duty to go. In the same serious, dedicated way, he has tried Yoga, Reichian and Jungian analysis, fasting and meditation, homosexuality, parachute jumping and autohypnosis — always carefully recording his sensations. Just as, two years ago here, when he learned that Charles Bell climbed a pine tree every morning before breakfast, Gerry felt he must also climb a pine tree, at least once.

While we were talking, Teddy and H. H. Waters came in. Teddy described the concert at Caroline's comically: everyone sitting around solemn and formal in her living room, listening to Teddy's tapes, which they didn't understand, and staring at Anna May (whom, Miss Waters says, they don't understand either??).

TEDDY: The truth is, as we all know, practically nobody can hear modern music except musicians. I know, Kenneth — you're one of the exceptions. But the ordinary educated person, even when he's quite advanced about art and literature, in music he usually hasn't got an inch past Bartók, and he never will. But they all think they've got to pretend.

It's sad, really. Caroline was listening, of course; she was the only one. Charlie just sat and suffered awful boredom for two hours. Ricky tried, though he knows the tapes already, but he kept being distracted by our Anna May, who was sitting literally at his feet in her yellow scoopneck dress. And poor Sally; *pangs* of jealousy.

Anna May completely neglected Charlie, he said, in favor of Ricky Potter. She hasn't much taste, was my first thought, to prefer that plumpish, puppyish boy – not boy to her, I suppose, as he's over thirty. But H. H. Waters pointed out, Ricky's the nearest thing here to an unattached young man. And probably, with the insensitivity of beauty (which is quite as blind as love), Anna May hasn't even registered Sally's existence, let alone her claim on Ricky.

Miss Waters also suggested a simpler and kinder explanation of tonight's seating plan: that Caroline asked Ricky and Charlie to sit with Anna May because they're the unattached men here nearest her age. I hadn't thought of that; marital status is still another of the divisions one forgets here ... But when someone from outside appears, they all spring back into existence – separating men from women, old from young, married from single. Rigid glass partitions, through which we can still see each other, but not hear very well; and never touch.

July 2

A simmering hot day, the grass steaming, the sun and everything beneath it foggy with haze. And I feel foggy myself: hot, blurred. I read my ghost story over again this morning, and I didn't like it. It seemed both trivial and pretentious; a thin, silly tale, elaborately overtold. Every sentence was like an awful parody of my work, artificially composed to deserve, in the worst sense, all the adjectives they used on the jacket of *At Home*:

> charming
> feminine
> witty
> sensitive
> subtle
> original

I'm reminded of the 'certain kind of woman' in the Peck & Peck ads, who has such charming, feminine, witty, etc., tastes, but always dresses with dowdy conventionality. One knows that her clothes tell the real truth, and her advertised enthusiasm for dandelions and French poetry is sheer affectation.

A letter from Clark in this morning's mail; all about Westford and problems there: Clarkie's complaints of day camp, the 'funny whining noise' Bessie claims she keeps hearing in the washer, a company dinner he had to attend alone. He also mentions that Professor Moore at Yale has invited him on an expedition to some place in Maine where a colony of rare marsh birds has been discovered. But since I am away, he says, he can't go.

I put the letter away and sat down to work on my story;

but domestic anxiety kept floating like a sticky mist between me and the paper. Suppose I tell Clark to have Bessie call the repairmen. They'll come and listen to the noise in the washer and go away again, and send us a bill for $6.50. Suppose I telephone home this afternoon, and ask Clarkie how camp is – he probably won't tell me, and if he realizes I'm worried about him it will upset him even more, if he really is upset. Etc.

And so all morning I've accomplished nothing.

Afternoon

A walk around the lake and lunch with Kenneth. Not so pleasant as it should have been; it was too hot in the woods and there were mosquitoes. He was pleased because he discovered some unusual and rather beautiful ferns; but I felt cross and itchy. And when we finally sat down on the bridge by the far lake and I opened my lunch box, all I found was a dry cheese sandwich and three hard oatmeal cookies. I suppose somebody else had my cottage cheese and fruit.

Kenneth pointed out what I should have seen before – that my depression about the story this morning was really backwash from Clark's letter. Guilt and self-doubt produced (perhaps deliberately) by his news about the washer, Clarkie, etc. 'The Right Sort of Wife doesn't leave when her washer is about to break down.' Or, possibly, 'If you were there, it wouldn't make that noise; it's whining for you to come home.' The statement about Clarkie is more complicated, something like 'The Right Sort of Mother is always on hand to listen to her children's problems, if they have any problems, which (with such a mother) they usually don't.'

Then the dinner party. Martie Murray, who is always talking about 'helping one's husband along,' would have said (I expect she did) that I should have been there. But Clark ought to understand. He would hate it really if I were one of those professional executive wives like Martie. Just as I'd hate it if he were one of those executive husbands like Steve Murray who rise as if they were ready-mixed biscuits out of a cardboard tube – and also become rock-hard as they cool. (I'd like to write about Steve and Martie; the exploitation of oneself as a natural resource, as bad as despoiling national parks – the story should make the connection – but of course I can't.)

Anyhow, as Kenneth pointed out, fretting about these domestic matters is not only wasteful; it's also a kind of cheating on Illyria.

KENNETH: After all, you weren't invited up here to worry about your washing machine. You're supposed to put all that out of your mind.

Even the nice parts of Clark's letter weren't, really. 'I certainly wish you were here.' (*And why aren't you?*) 'I hope you're having a good time and getting a real rest.' (*You're there to sleep and enjoy/indulge yourself, not to do anything important.*) And at once I feel discouraged and hopeless, because I know that whatever I have to show him when I get home, Clark won't think much of it. 'That seems all right to me,' he always says. 'Of course, it's not the sort of thing I would ordinarily read.' (Quite true. He reads political commentary, natural history, occasionally a spy story.)

And the business about the bird-watching expedition is almost certainly deliberate. Clark isn't really that eager to spend all next weekend in some dismal wet swamp in Maine, any more than he is to leave Westford Casualty and write a book on bird migration. He likes to talk about it, but he has no intention of doing anything so quixotic. Not because he is so devoted to the company. He doesn't care for most of his colleagues, or really enjoy either the exercise of authority or material success. Unlike most people, he isn't interested in living pleasantly, being able to buy beautiful things and travel abroad; in fact, being something of a Puritan, he rather distrusts pleasure and beauty and abroad. What he values is order and security – and therefore he values his job, which can *insure* these things.

In more than one sense, as I said to Kenneth, Clark is an 'insurance man.' In every situation he calculates the odds, and prepares for the worst. Partly, I think, it's the result of having grown up in the Depression. (So did I, but I was five years younger and didn't notice so much. Besides, we weren't really much affected. The Stockwells lost nearly everything – not that they didn't get it back, and more, afterward.) Even when we first met, Clark had a streak of cautious pessimism. I thought then it would wear off as he became more secure, but instead it's grown wider.

I suppose an insurance company naturally attracts and/or creates men whose temperamental inclination is toward caution – anticipating difficulties, not taking chances, hedging their bets. It's a bad business really: the encouragement of cowardice and fear. Those pamphlets Clark's department puts out to remind people of possible disasters: fire, flood, failure; sickness, accident and death. I remember especially the color photograph on the cover of a recent one: four men with briefcases have suddenly appeared on the front lawn of a modest suburban home, all wearing raincoats, though it is not raining. The young couple just getting out of their station wagon with two small children looks at them apprehensively as they stand on the bright green grass by the white picket fence, each holding his hat in his hand and smiling faintly. Four messengers of ill fortune: underwriters, undertakers.

A story about insurance men – an insurance man. I can't write it, but someone should.

On our way back from lunch Kenneth and I walked around by the pool. It's usually deserted by two o'clock, but today Leonard, Charlie, Ricky Potter and Anna May were still there. We sat down with them for a bit, feeling like children playing hookey. As Leonard said, we all kept expecting Caroline Kent to appear and scold us for not being back at work. (At this, everyone looked nervously toward the shrubbery.) She wouldn't need to scold, actually; her mere appearance would be enough.

Demonstrative anecdote: A month or so ago, according to Charlie, a bunch of young hoods from the city drove up here and got into Illyria late one night. They climbed the wall somehow, and Louis (the night watchman) found them out by the pool about two AM, drinking beer and shouting and splashing water. When he told them to leave, they refused; they were coarse and insulting – one of them threatened him with a knife. Then they tried to throw him into the pool, but Louis broke away and ran back to the Lodge, locked himself in, and telephoned Caroline. She didn't call the police – just got up and dressed and left the house. She walked over to the pool alone (Louis was afraid to accompany her), and asked the hoods if they would please go now, because they were disturbing her guests. They apologized and left.

Anna May didn't join in our conversation, only lay sunning herself in a deck chair, now and then rubbing on oil until she was as golden brown, smooth and glossy as expensive fresh-baked pastry. She paid almost no attention to Leonard, Charlie or Ricky – or to us. The more intelligent and lively we all were, the more we gestured and smiled and spoke about art, the less she responded.

As I was wondering about this and trying to account for it, a strange thing happened. Suddenly, for a moment, I saw Anna May's companions as they must have looked to her, through her oversized dark glasses. Stripped of their clothes, her idealized artists had become three aging, inferior specimens. Ricky was a foolish bright pink on one side from the sun, too plump all over, and going bald too soon. Leonard was distastefully thin and wrinkled and hairy – his long sinewy legs and arms covered with something like steel wool. And poor Charlie, who's too fair to tan, looked like something found under a rock – or rather under a big damp white towel, from which emerged only some knobby pale feet and a nose painted zinc-white. What I'd seen a moment before as three interesting, attractive men, now hardly looked human. They were like animals in disguise: a pig, a monkey and an old white horse, in circus bathing costumes.

Then Nick Donato appeared from the pool house. Through Anna May's sunglasses his vulgarity was invisible. The sideburns and too-long shiny black hair, the shiny red nylon bathing trunks, were filtered out. All that remained was a well-muscled, well-tanned man with a marked air of physical confidence and energy. Anna May registered these facts, for her eyes, even her head, turned, following Nick as he dived from the board; as he surfaced, snorting and shaking off water, and then swam several lengths of the pool, splashing noisily. When he finally stopped, resting one elbow on the gutter and grinning across at us, Anna May sat up, grinned back and waved for him to come over.

More trouble with the ghost story. All this afternoon I was working on it, rearranging and rewriting sentences, but not improving them; it still reads like Peck & Peck.

I don't know what's the matter with me; it was all right at first; or at least better. And before when I've been here I just sat down and wrote all day, stopping only to thank God or Caroline silently for the opportunity. It never occurred to me that if one weren't working well, everything good about Illyria would turn upside down. Now the continual beauty and abundance begin to make me feel guilty; the carefully arranged silence becomes a silent accusation; and Caroline Kent's genuine solicitude for my welfare is genuinely oppressive. Even when she's not around, there are those signs everywhere, in a fine, elegant black Edwardian typescript that seems to imitate her voice. 'Please Observe Quiet in the Hallways. Others Are Working.' (*Why Aren't You?*)

Later

A peaceful evening. The croquet game broke up early because Charlie, Ricky and Nick were taking Anna May to the early show of a movie in Jerico. On this visit, it seems, Caroline isn't going to chaperone her so carefully. Perhaps she thinks Anna May's old enough now to take care of herself.

What Anna May thinks is impossible to determine. If she prefers Nick, it didn't show at supper, when her child-like admiration, quite revived, shone on all three of them impartially. A concession to ward off Caroline's anxiety? A merely flirtatious maneuver? Or does she really admire all artists (at least when clothed) alike?

The rest of us worked or read for a while after supper and then met for beer at the pool house. Since it's got so warm, that's the pleasantest place.

We talked, inevitably, about Anna May. Everyone (except Sally Sachs, who sat sunk in misery, hardly speaking or moving the whole time except to pull open beer cans with an angry jerk) has a different theory. Mine is, as I said before, that she acts as a sort of unconscious chemical filter to separate the serious artists here from those who can be distracted from their work with comparative ease. One can almost imagine Caroline inviting her partly for this purpose.

Leonard objected; perhaps he thought I was excluding him because I used the word 'artists,' though I certainly hadn't meant to – if anything, I meant to flatter all of us there. He declared that Anna May was an anti-Semite – which seemed so improbable an explanation of her behavior that I laughed out loud. The faces of everyone present (except Kenneth) showed that I shouldn't have. Suddenly they all had the same sour, wry expression – as if Leonard, Gerry, Sally, even Teddy Berg, had simultaneously put on identical rubber Jewish masks.

LEONARD: You think that's funny, Janet?

JANET: No. But I don't think it's so. I only laughed because it seemed so unlikely.

LEONARD: Unlikely? To me, it seems obvious. What else have Baxter and Porter and Donato got in common, except that they're all goys?

I should have realized Leonard was sensitive on this subject, because only last month I read his piece in *Harper's* on 'The Jewish Novel and Its Critics.' I should have remembered that, but I was too infatuated with my own theory.

And now I suppose he at least, if not the others, thinks *I'm* anti-Semitic. The trouble is, once they think that, anything one might say to refute it only makes it worse. 'As a matter of fact, at home I'm on the Board of ...' No. So I said nothing, which didn't help much either.

So now I've inadvertently made an enemy, or at least an unfriend, of somebody I really like, and who I believe liked me – before Anna May came. And he's a well-known critic and book reviewer too, I can't help thinking.

Teddy and Gerry, though they accepted the idea that Anna May was prejudiced, didn't give it much weight. 'What else could you expect, with her background?' (suburban Long Island). She seemed fickle and flirtatious to us, Teddy said, mainly because of the difference in age.

TEDDY: You've all got to remember, she's still more or less a child. Eager, enthusiastic – but with a veryvery short attention span by your adult standards.

I was ready to admit this, but the others looked doubtful, and Gerry openly disagreed. He thinks that what attracts Anna May isn't novelty, but artistic prestige. In other words, she isn't a chick of the ordinary fluffy Easter basket sort, but belongs to a different subspecies – more calculating and not at all naïve, with its eye and claw out for the main chance. He claims she only paid so much attention to Ricky last night because she'd heard Teddy say he was a brilliant young composer. Then at breakfast this morning Charlie happened to make a joke about how famous Nick is, so now she's after him.

Prestige, fame. It's something one doesn't think of often here, blessedly. Illyria makes that easy, by treating all its guests alike. But of course one *could* classify them.

There are three groups, really. First, those whose names are known to the general public, the ordinary educated person. Theodore Berg, H. H. Waters. Possibly L. D. Zimmern and Nick Donato too, but with a difference. The first two are stable, long-established reputations. A book has been published about Harmonia, many articles. Even if she should never write another word, she's sure of a place in American literary history. Teddy's fame is even greater, though less explicit. Everyone knows that he changed the course of modern music, but even here at Illyria probably no one but Ricky (and possibly Caroline) could tell you exactly how he did it.

Leonard's position as an important critic is more recent – only about five years old. Nick's fame is even newer, and less secure. Eighteen months ago, nobody had ever heard of him. Then suddenly his work was being pictured in *Life* and *Newsweek*, attacked in the *Times*, bought up by important collectors, etc. It's really not very good, Kenneth thinks, though it brings high prices at the moment: full of cheap shock effects, childish colors and images. People will soon tire of it, he predicts, and in a year or so, like others before him, Nick will sink back into obscurity almost as fast as he rose from it.

The second level of prestige here is made up of those of us who are known mainly within our own profession. We are the middle class of Illyria, the solid citizens. Most American poets must know of Gerry Grass, and most painters of Kenneth (who also has considerable reputation as a teacher). And I suppose most short-story writers will have heard of me, at least vaguely – because one keeps up with the competition.

All of us, in some private room of our minds, still hope for more: for real fame, for a sudden visit from the muse of the first-rate. But we have more or less (according to our age and character) given up *expecting* it. Kenneth knows that he's a very good painter, but not a great one; while Gerry still visibly barks and pants after fame, like a golden retriever after a speeding sports car. He may catch her yet – he's only thirty-four. The trouble is, most of his audience is much younger than that. They trust him now, though he's over thirty – but how long will they go on trusting him?

Then there are Sally and Ricky. They're probably already heroes to their friends and families, but hardly anyone else has ever heard of them. Ricky, who's still young, will probably go further; so may Sally – though Kenneth doubts it. But theoretically, either of them might end up famous.

Charlie, I suppose, is in a category by himself. He was certainly in Group I once. But now I wonder whether any American novelist, making a list of important living American novelists, would include his name – twenty years is a long time. So he's not really in Group II either. And he's forty-seven. If he's in Group III, the odds are heavy against him; and he knows it.

But at Illyria, in the society of his peers, Charlie can believe he's still going to make it. And maybe he is: Leonard thinks it's a possibility, since he's seen part of Charlie's novel. Usually Charlie won't show his work to anyone, but Anna May somehow persuaded him to lend her the first section; and this morning she went around with it to Leonard's studio.

LEONARD: I didn't feel too good about it. A first-person narrative of the Indian wars; well, I expected something discouraging. So I told her I didn't want to read it without Baxter's permission, but she pouted and coaxed and insisted he wouldn't mind. Actually it was interesting. Not at all what I'd expected, but very interesting.

There is a special gesture Leonard makes when he's delivering a professional judgement, and a special expression. He drops and protrudes his jaw slightly, and thumps with the side of his fist upon the table, or on his knee, to emphasize his deliberately chosen words. And though he looks solemn, really he's quite pleased with himself.

All of us feel better about our work at Illyria; calmer, more serious, more able to experiment. Leonard can think beyond next week's review; Gerry next week's poem. Charlie can escape from his failure, and Teddy from his success – both from the temptation to repeat himself, and from what he called 'the dirty social backwash of fame.'

This social aspect of fame is disturbing. Even in very small quantities. Like last fall when *At Home* came out and there was that imitation party at the bookstore; and I was interviewed on the radio and for that silly article on the woman's page of the local paper. I would have preferred to find I despised and deplored these things, and was only doing them because my publisher wanted it, as I pretended (to myself as well as to others). Or if I hadn't the moral strength for that position, I would at least have liked to take a simple egoistic pleasure in the situation.

Instead I found that I had become consciously and nervously ambivalent about being recognized in local shops, seeing a magazine which I knew had a review in it on someone's coffee table, etc. Even now, whenever I go into a bookstore in Westford, I can't help looking for *At Home* first. If it's still there, well out in front, I'm embarrassed and edge off sideways from it. I wouldn't want to touch the thing; I hardly dare look in that direction again for fear of being caught in the act. But if they don't have it, I feel vacant and hurt.

I was talking to Teddy about this while the others played ping-pong, and describing some of the poison-gas effects of the book on my acquaintances in Westford. I suppose I thought he was so far above such problems, so used to fame, that he would be sympathetic. Instead he turned rather waspish.

TEDDY: Janet, m'dear, I don't think you're so very embarrassed and overwhelmed by all this public response. I think you're really a wee bit cross there hasn't been more ... Of course I'm speaking from my own experience. But what I remember best about my first success is how awfully disappointed I was. I had lots of fan letters, and inquiries from record companies, and offers to play my pieces all over the country, and everyone was telling me how good I must feel. But what I secretly thought, way down inside, was 'Is this all?' ... We artists are such awful egotists. Because what I'd really wanted, and even expected, was that the whole *world* would love me; and you know, it didn't at all.

I would hate to admit, and didn't admit to Teddy, that I was like that. But there is a sort of truth in what he says. For nearly twenty years I did think, in a kind of indefinite way, that if I published a book, 'everything would be all right.' I believed it just as girls believe they will live happily ever after the wedding. (I thought that once, too.) I did vaguely imagine that the world would love me better – and when it turned out instead that most of the world didn't notice, and the rest, if anything, loved me somewhat less, I felt cheated.

I'm annoyed with Teddy too because he refused to help Sally Sachs, or even take her misery seriously.

JANET: You protected Sally from Nick; why don't you do something now to protect Ricky from Anna May?

TEDDY: Because he doesn't need protection. What he needs, as I said, is emotional experience.

JANET: But how about Sally? Just look at her: slamming the ball in that wild way. Anyone can see she feels horrible.

TEDDY: She'll get over it. Anna May will be gone in a few days, and Sally will think the better of Ricky for her having been interested in him. Just as we all do.

So even Teddy, who considers her such a child, is influenced by Anna May's opinions.

At ten o'clock – almost as if to prove Gerry right in his view of Anna May, and the rest of us wrong – she appeared at the pool house. 'Oh, there you are!' she shrieked musically at Leonard. 'Aunt Caroline said you might be over here. You've got to come along back to the house – we need you for bridge. Charlie's quit and Nick can't play.' I saw, or imagined I saw, an internal struggle; Leonard made some wisecrack – but he finally got up and came along. Kenneth said charitably afterward that he hadn't wanted to displease 'Aunt Caroline.' But I'm not so sure. I think Aunt Caroline was an excuse, and Leonard knew she was an excuse.

I suppose one shouldn't be surprised. The truth is that whatever they may say, most men are weak where a pretty girl is concerned. Only those who are really grown-up, like Kenneth – or as confident of themselves and happily married as Gerry – remain immune.

July 3

An uncomfortable morning. Nearly everyone's in a bad mood: the servants because they have extra work getting things ready for the concert tonight; Caroline concerned that it should go off perfectly; and half the guests upset by Anna May.

Both Charlie and Nick now seem to be in disfavor. ('Oh come *on*, don't let's sit there,' I heard her say to Leonard as we were getting our coffee at breakfast. And they went over to Ricky's table by the window, ignoring Charlie's smiles and waves.) Has someone broken the news to her that Charlie's a literary failure, and Nick only a fly-by-night success – or is it just childish capriciousness?

It's hard to say which one is taking it worse: Nick, who's obviously not used to any sort of rejection; or Charlie, who is. Unfortunately, neither of them has the strength to ignore her; though grudgingly, they continue to wag their tails and snap their jaws whenever she looks their way or throws them a morsel of attention.

But the attention of an Anna May has terribly insidious effects. She begins by generously showering every artist she meets with – at the time, I think, quite sincere – interest and awe. This is what they have always hoped for from the public – or secretly felt they deserved. They become drunk on it; then addicted. Overnight they begin to do things for her they wouldn't do for anyone else: Nick agreed to let her pose for him, Charlie showed her his play, and Leonard has promised to drive into Jerico this morning so he can give her a copy of his book on American Realism, which she will probably never read. Of course the more they attend to Anna May the less time they have for their work, setting up a vicious spiral, since it's their work that makes them interesting to her. (I think it's quite possible that Anna May loses interest in anyone who seems to have nothing better to do than follow her around.) Meanwhile, her admiration has become a proof of their artistic success and ability, so its withdrawal is deeply depressing. The history of the Artist and the World in miniature.

Ricky's in favor, so Sally is tense and miserable (especially since it came out at breakfast that he's giving Anna May a recording which he promised to Sally earlier). But he has stiff competition now from Leonard, which makes *him* tense and miserable. Kenneth, Teddy, Gerry and I are annoyed too, because all our friends are making fools of themselves.

The program for the concert, engraved like a wedding announcement, was posted on the bulletin board after breakfast, next to a typed notice instructing us how to behave tonight. Mozart, Debussy, Beethoven. Dinner is to be served half an hour early, and 'guests are requested to vacate the first floor of the Mansion' directly afterward. We are also requested to 'avoid typing, playing records, or having loud conversation in the rooms and corridors,' and to make all our telephone calls from the Lodge. We don't get to go to the concert, because 'space is regretfully limited.' (Tickets are fifty dollars each, for the benefit of a projected nearby arts center.) However, we may sit in the upstairs hall and hear the trio; the doors to the music room will be left open on purpose.

Actually, Kenneth says, a few of us *have* been invited to the concert: Teddy, and Harmonia Waters, and also Charlie (he is ushering). Caroline apologized to Kenneth for not having a seat for him, but unfortunately/fortunately they are sold out. It's really too bad – this being the sort of music he likes most.

Then on top of everything else, there was a quarrel at breakfast between Charlie and Leonard, with some dam-

70

age to the bystanders (me). Quite gratuitous, since *until Anna May came* we all got on well.

Anna May had just left (with Ricky, to visit his studio, which I suppose partly explains it); Leonard, deserted, brought his coffee over to the table where Charlie, Nick and I were sitting. It was Nick who began it really, with some crack about Anna May – asking how Leonard had made out with her last night, though it was clear that he hadn't. Charlie laughed and repeated the question, with a kind of sour pleasure I've never seen in him before; and Leonard muttered some joke to the effect that he was still doing better than Charlie.

Charlie didn't answer, but a kind of flu seemed to have got into the room. I knew something disagreeable was going to happen; and presently Charlie began talking in a suspiciously light voice about a review of Leonard's he'd read, and saying that some opinion in it was just what one would expect from a critic. So Leonard asked what he had against critics. Did he think they'd treated him unfairly? In a moment they were at it – laughing a lot and pretending to be kidding, but really not.

CHARLIE: I don't have anything against critics. I just think they might wait until we're dead to tear us apart. And meantime have the decency to stay out of our way.
LEONARD: I suppose you mean, stay out of Illyria?
CHARLIE: No, not necessarily. When Carlos and Dorothy were around last year working on Hemingway, that was okay.
LEONARD: Critics are okay, as long as they aren't critical of you.
CHARLIE: That's right. Frankly, I don't know what Caroline was thinking of, asking someone like you up here.

Pretending to smile, they glared at each other, but in different styles. Rage exaggerates people idiosyncratically: all of Leonard seemed to tighten and draw in on itself; his wiry hair curled even tighter. Charlie, on the other hand, appeared to stretch, and become more pale and vertical than before; *his* hair (he kept running his hand through it as he spoke) got long and stringy, like faded dead grass.

Nick and I both tried to make peace, but we only got bruised.

NICK: Aw, come off it. Why the hell shouldn't she? Maybe she thought it would be some use to him. Or to the rest of you writers, having a guy around who –

CHARLIE: Oh, yeah. How would you like having Clement Greenberg around here?

Unfair, since Leonard likes Charlie's work; whereas Greenberg (according to Kenneth) has cited Nick as an example of all that is most deplorable in modern American art. Nick took it well, but Charlie, with shreds of hay flopping about over his forehead, and a tense smile twitching between every two sentences, went right on.

NICK: Hell, as long as he left *me* alone –

CHARLIE: But he wouldn't; that's the point. Listen, letting someone like Greenberg or Zimmern into Illyria, it's just not sporting. It's like letting a hunter into a wildlife sanctuary.

JANET: Oh, now, really, it seems to me this is a large enough place so that one –

CHARLIE: In the city you've got a chance, but here you can't get away from him. He's always sneaking up and firing questions at you about the moral and philosophical meaning of your work. Or, What do you think is the main weakness of your last book, please? Answer that, Janet.

JANET: Well, I –

LEONARD: If I'd thought you were so threatened by our conversation about your manuscript yesterday, I wouldn't have asked to see the rest of it. If you want it back ...

CHARLIE: No, go ahead; read it. I already know what you're going to say.

By this time the air was thick with flu. I tried to disinfect it: I made some remark about how everyone was edgy today, and how well we all get on usually, but it didn't work. Charlie became sulkily mute, and both Leonard and Nick turned on me.

JANET: When you consider that what one's got here is a houseful of people who make their living looking at things differently from everyone else, professional individualists ... Really, it's remarkable how little trouble there is, most of the time.

LEONARD: But we're doing our best to start some.

JANET: Well, you are rather, today.

LEONARD: Janet doesn't like arguments. She wants everybody to get on nicely all the time in school and not fight.

JANET: No, but I do think that when one's been invited here, one is responsible, after all –

NICK: Hey! You know something? Janet has an imaginary friend named Wun. An Oriental. She's always telling us his opinions. 'Wun prefers the kind of art Wun was brought up on. Wun is *responsible*, after all.'

Everybody laughed at this, and felt better again. Except me. I've accused Anna May of bringing out the worst in people, one way or another – just as Illyria brings out the best in them. But in some cases the worst is fairly easy to bring out: the vanity, childishness and aggression are near the surface, only thinly overlaid with charm or good manners. In someone like Nick Donato, hardly overlaid at all.

I expect what they said is so, all the same. I *do* want people to get on with each other – and why not?

And I do use the impersonal pronoun a good deal. In my writing, especially. I generalize my observations, my opinions – announcing, as it were, that they're shared by an imaginary One, Two, Three, Four others; gently inviting the reader to be of our number. But is that really illegitimate, wrong, a trick? Isn't all writing a trick, doesn't one – that is, rather, don't I – Oh, bah.

And I use him, too, to give my emotions a larger, more Olympian dignity. One is irritated, or One is depressed, but – like other deities – never without good reason.

I just read over my new story, in imagination changing One to I throughout. A tedious character appeared, sententious, supersensitive –

Ah, *hell*.

After lunch

I couldn't work at all this AM, shut alone in my room with Wun, so I went out for a long walk through the woods. Coming back, I met H. H. Waters in the vegetable garden (eating raw peas off the vine), and she invited me to have lunch with her. I felt shy again, but it turned out well. One of the best conversations about writing I've ever had. Maybe because HHW (I still can't bring myself to call her 'Harmonia,' so I stupidly don't call her anything) knows what it's like to be a 'lady writer.'

I've complained of Clark that he thinks literature just a rather eccentric hobby for a housewife. But everyone here, even Kenneth, tends to speak of my life in Westford as if it were a rather eccentric hobby for a writer. Since it seems to interfere with my work, why don't I give it up? They don't see what HHW sees at once, that it's the essential substance of my work, without which there wouldn't be any Janet Belle Smith, or any stories.

Really, most people don't like the idea of a serious woman writer, or find it incongruous. They prefer to forget either that you're a writer or that you're a woman – 'The usual choice, in my case,' she said wryly. As a result, it's reported in interviews that HHW can make peach pie, as if this were a most peculiar, original circumstance.

74

I was still so preoccupied with Wun that I told her what Nick had said. She laughed, but understood. She hadn't had so much trouble with him, she said; her problem was on a more primitive religious level. She'd found out that if she didn't watch herself she began anthropomorphizing everything in nature – clouds, frogs, leaves, rain; twigs and pebbles even – 'in the most insidious, cloying way.' And she said, which may be true, that my best stories probably didn't have Wun in them. (But if so, my best stories were all written over five years ago.)

I also tried to tell her what I've been feeling this spring, that there's something boring about my writing. H. H. Waters didn't have any advice, but she sympathized, and told a nice anecdote about how she first started writing poetry. She was a sophomore in high school; her English teacher had assigned a composition, and she couldn't think of an idea. She was sitting in the hanging swing on the front porch, complaining of this to her uncle, who had just come out for a smoke, when the cleaners' delivery truck went by on the street. Her uncle waved his hand at the truck and said, 'Why don't you write about that?'

HARMONIA: Well, I thought, Oh Lord, he just doesn't understand at all. But I wanted to be polite, so I said, 'You mean I should make up a story about the fellow who drives that truck, about his job or his family, or some funny incident that could happen to him when he delivers his next bundle?' And Uncle Jacob said, no, he meant I should write about how we saw the truck go by, and what it looked like, and what he said and what I said and what we thought about it.

And so her story turned into a poem.

But I'm not a poet. I haven't the musical sense, or the sense of perfection. In a poem, each word has to be right and contribute to the whole; in a story only every sentence. In a novel, only every page.

Preparations for the concert tonight have already

begun, I could hardly get back into the Mansion; the door was blocked by a moving van, with sweaty dark men carrying in stacks of gilt chairs and cartons of glass and china. The carpet in the main hall was covered with a canvas drop cloth, and a plumber was trying to get the fountain working. All he had produced so far was a slow pathetic drip and trickle, as if the fat marble cherub poised above the marble bowl had a bad runny nose. Meanwhile Charlie was hurrying from room to room, with large pale gestures showing the moving men where to set things down; then changing his mind, dashing back out toward the truck –

Another 'delivery truck.' A sign? Should I write about Charlie, then? I can imagine a theme: the artist who had and still has talent, but can't successfully order the gross natural world any longer. Parallel: his delicately minor recent poems – glass, fine china, gilt bentwood.

But I don't want to do that. I think writers must grant one another professional immunity. And I certainly don't want to write about the moving men or the plumber, invent *their* lives and perceptions, of which I really know nothing. That would be false social realism, or at best false pastoral.

Later

Kenneth just came around to find out where I'd been at lunchtime. I hadn't said I'd meet him at the pool, but he'd taken it for granted I'd be there as usual, especially since it was so warm.

The annoying truth is that since Anna May arrived I haven't been swimming – and not because I don't want to swim, but because I haven't wanted to show myself in a bathing suit. I walked over to the pool again late yesterday afternoon with the idea of having a dip before supper. Anna May wasn't there, only Gerry and Ricky Potter. It was hot, the water looked wonderfully cool and wet; my suit was hanging in the dressing room – but I didn't go in. I stood around making conversation and looking at the pool as if it were a block of lime jello without any practical function.

It's not Anna May's own scorn I'm afraid of – though I'm sure she would regard me with scorn, as another scrawny old animal like Charlie and Leonard. What I mind is the idea of letting the others see me suspended in the jello, as naked as a slice of fruit, letting them coolly compare my body with hers.

Of course any woman of my age might feel this; but what's so irritating is that I should feel it enough now to give up swimming. After all, we go to the pool at the country club nearly every weekend, and it's always full of handsome young people. But Clark doesn't really look at them – or if he does, I know he won't compare us to my real disadvantage. He's satisfied that his wife should be neat, elegant and respectably attractive for her age. If she resembled Anna May he would be embarrassed, even annoyed.

Another depressing thing: I tried to talk to Kenneth about how my work isn't going well again, and he didn't understand. When I said that my recent stories, including the current one, seem unoriginal and even unreal to me, he just thought I was being an oversensitive Lady Writer. He tried to reassure me, saying he far preferred them to the earlier ones, because they were 'so beautifully written.'

JANET: Yes – maybe. But good writing isn't everything.
KENNETH: What more would you like? Social significance? You sound as if you'd been listening to Charlie Baxter. I remember back in the thirties when I first went to New York, the WPA artists used to talk that sort of nonsense. 'Oh, yah, Cezanne's a good painter, but good painting isn't everything.'

Something occurred to me, though I didn't want to say it: that Kenneth too is beginning to repeat, almost to imitate, himself. His recent pictures are like my stories:

beautifully painted but not very original any more. Hills and roads and woods and clouds delicately indicated and subtly – but a little monotonously – distinguished.

Or maybe that's just my depression.

'You missed an interesting scene out at the pool,' Kenneth said. 'Anna May kidnapped Gerry. She sort of swooped down on him and announced that she'd persuaded Caroline to let her have the best-looking man at Illyria to escort her to the concert tonight.' I suppose Gerry could hardly have refused this invitation without insulting both Anna May and Caroline; but Kenneth says he didn't even seem to consider refusing it.

Why would Gerry bother with Anna May? I suppose because, according to his theory, her interest proves him a success; it also proves he's trusted by people under thirty. And not only is he going to the concert with her – since he doesn't have any evening clothes, they are driving to the nearest city this afternoon (over thirty miles) to rent some for him.

It's a disagreeable joke that the most anti-establishment artist here should give up a whole afternoon of his life, and whatever he might have accomplished in it, so he can attend a society party in correct formal dress. But the truth is, despite their initial protestations, Anna May has in a few days seduced them all. First Charlie and Ricky; next Nick, then Leonard, finally even Gerry.

Not really seduced – that one might understand and excuse, given the situation here. She has merely interrupted their work, exploited their energy and attention. If Caroline *did* introduce her into Illyria as a sort of litmus paper, then all of them have turned pink, failed the seriousness test. Leonard didn't get back to his studio all morning; Ricky's piano was silent out in the woods.

Meanwhile, I can't write. Sally goes on painting, but Kenneth says she's overworking terribly and ruining everything. She does delicate abstracts, rose and brown predominating. Now, he reports, it's as if she'd scratched them all over with a knife, or her fingernails, and they were weeping, mud running down their faces. And Sally looks bad herself – all lumpy and heavy, with her hair in her eyes, just as Teddy said she was when she first arrived.

The Concert

It was an occasion. I'm glad to have been here for it – not only to have heard the trio, which was very fine, but to have seen Illyria as it must have been in its prime, over fifty years ago. Because of course the Illyria we know now is half-asleep, or more than half – under a kind of spell.

Tonight for a few hours it came awake again. The stones blocking the driveway to the front of the house had been rolled away; the iron gates unchained; the Tiffany lanterns lit beside the front door and the heavy bolts drawn back. Inside the hall the fountain was turned full on; the cherub's perfunctory sniffle had become a glittering cascade of laughter. Freed from their muslin covers, the chairs and sofas looked like great fat furred animals, all velvet brocade and gilt fringe; and every light was on – from the ruby and rhinestone chandeliers overhead to the low wall sconces with their pink flame-shaped bulbs. Everything post-1910, everything functional and modern, had been put away; the stainless-steel tableware we use, the utility glassware and ashtrays had been replaced with silver and crystal. White damask covered the tables, and there were flowers and candles everywhere.

The cars which began to arrive about eight were of course recent models – mostly chauffeur-driven Cadillacs and Lincolns, or sports cars of exotic brands which Leonard identified for us. But the people who alighted from them could have passed as Undine Moffat's contemporaries. The men were in evening clothes, and some (including the musicians) in tails; and there were no minidresses – it was all long gowns of chiffon, lace and watered satin; pale fur wraps; and more (presumably real) jewelry than I've seen in an age – since my last opening night at the Cleveland Symphony; in fact, before I was married.

And then I realized what was strange was that I wasn't down there among those people, all of whom I knew so well as types – and a few I even knew as individuals: the Robert Palmers were there, and Aunt Peg's friend Isabel Halstead, who (now that I think of it) has a summer place near Jerico. That if this concert had been held in Cleveland, or in Westford, I might have attended it. But also that it was rather fun in a way not to be down there all dressed up for once, but instead watching from behind the scenes. (If I *had* been downstairs, there would have been a moment of embarrassment. 'Why, Janet Smith!' I can hear Mrs Halstead say. 'What are you doing here, dear? ... You mean *you're* one of the *artists*?')

As the concert didn't start until nine, we all might have gone to our rooms and worked, but no one could. Instead we stood at the front windows of the Mansion watching the cars drive up, and then hurried to the back to look down at the ladies and gentlemen walking foreshortened on the terrace below us, and pointed out eccentricities of dress and appearance to one another as children do.

Children was exactly what we were like – what we're always like at Illyria, but it took the concert to make it obvious. Physically, because the house and grounds are so large that the scale of childhood is restored: lawns it takes ten minutes to cross, giant trees, doors almost too heavy to push open, ceilings three times one's own height, huge rooms, massive furniture – even the bathrooms are twice the normal size. Socially too, because we have no duties here except a few chores like keeping our rooms neat, but must obey a number of rules: eat what's put before us or go hungry, stay out of certain parts of the house and grounds at certain hours, and try not to bother the servants or the grownups (Paula and Caroline). And when there's a party, we're not allowed downstairs – though some of the guests will politely ask after us, and admire the drawings of the most artistically gifted boys and girls on display in the little gallery.

We're so used to being treated this way that it didn't occur to anyone to resent it until nearly at the end of the evening. We hung over the banisters and longed for the sandwiches and cakes and ices we could see on display below; we were excited and pleased when Caroline sent a waiter in a red coat up to us with glasses of real champagne on a silver tray. After the audience had gone into the music room, we all settled ourselves obediently at the top of the grand staircase, on the broad crimson-carpeted steps, to listen.

The only trouble was, we couldn't hear very well, even when we crept down as far as the landing and sat on the long bench under the stained-glass window (glossy and dark now, like oily water at night). Even Ricky, though he knew the music well, was straining; and H. H. Waters, who's slightly deaf, gave up almost at once. (HHW had been invited to attend the concert, but declined. 'If I had to go into that crowd of strange people,' she told us, 'I'd have heard even less.' I was thinking of leaving myself when Kenneth suggested we might do better outdoors.

So he and I sneaked down the back stairs and around the front of the house, unseen except by a bored chauffeur or two, like children out after their bedtime. It was almost night by now, the sky a saturated blue, the pines inky dark against it. Where the light from the windows fanned out, the lawn looked unreal, artificially green.

As soon as we got around the house we could hear the trio. We hurried across the grass, up the stone steps of the terrace, and sat on the wall outside the music room, in the shadow between two fans of light. The doors onto the terrace had been shut again, but we could hear perfectly through the transom of the nearest window. They were playing Debussy: the piano very liquid, the cello buzzing like a great bee. There was a little cool breeze, but the stone was still quite warm, and we sat close together.

After the Debussy came intermission. The audience

stood up and moved around: we saw them in indistinct colored mosaic through the leaded windows, which have a heraldic motif in the center of each pane, surrounded by alternate plain and colored blocks of glass. So, as they moved, their faces and limbs were dyed sea-green and musty gold, or shone pale and warped as if under water, like ghosts – the ghosts of an evening sixty years ago.

When they emerged into the hall, where the windows have only a colored border, we could see them better. Teddy appeared first, giggling with someone; Charlie Baxter looking handsome, nervous and pale in his evening clothes; the Palmers; and a crowd of prosperous, pow-dered, dressed-up people. Finally Anna May came out, in a cerise strapless satin evening gown, holding up her train with one arm and clinging to Gerry (very elegant in his rented clothes) with the other. Ridiculously overdressed, I thought her. Kenneth didn't agree – or rather he agreed, but somehow found it touching.

KENNETH: Anna May looks charming, doesn't she? ... Don't you think so?
JANET: I think she looks a little silly. That dress is all wrong – much too old and sophisticated for her. She's like a child in her mother's evening gown, trying to act sophisticated and holding up the hem so she won't trip.
KENNETH: But that's the charm of it. In that dress, and especially among that crowd, Anna May's obviously out of place – so young and innocent.
JANET: You really think she's innocent? After the way she's made up to everyone here?
KENNETH: That's how I *know* she's innocent. If she weren't she wouldn't flirt so openly. It's all play-acting.

A few members of the audience came to the door and gazed out idly, but (as if *we* were ghosts) they didn't seem to see us sitting on the wall in the shadows. And suddenly there was Caroline Kent, in ice-gray silk and a diamond choker, with her hair elaborately arranged. She also looked out, right at us; but she didn't see us either – or, with ice-gray-silk calm, gave no sign that she had.

The best piece on the program was after intermission: Beethoven's Trio in D Major. They played it beautifully. At least, they played the first movement beautifully; we missed the rest. Sitting by the window nearest us was a henlike elderly lady in pink ruched chiffon and diamonds, who kept fretfully adjusting a net stole around her shoulders and whispering to the elderly man next to her. When the first movement was over, he got up and shut the transom. Clank. And sat down again. The musicians continued playing; we could see them moving their hands behind the colored glass. Only now we couldn't hear anything. We had to sneak back around into the house again, and upstairs, and strain to listen again with the rest.

But this time feeling angry, cheated. The idea that we could be so blandly shut out – that someone who cares as much about good music as Kenneth does, or even a composer like Ricky, couldn't hear the concert decently, while all those overdressed philistines – (Of course I know Mrs Halstead cares about music, and there must have been others like her, though not many; but I'd forgotten about Mrs Halstead, and was as angry as the rest of them.) As Charlie would have said, and could have said if he'd been with us and not dressed up as a penguin downstairs, so Leonard said it for him: 'Why are you so surprised? That's how the world always treats its intellectuals. That's what they really think of us.'

The worst of it isn't the antagonism we felt for the audience, though, but the resentment toward our fellow guests: Charlie, Gerry, even Teddy. I hate finding out that artists are frauds – that all Gerry's hippie philosophy and Charlie's radical politics, so eloquently expressed, couldn't keep them away from this demonstration of established power and privilege. That Illyria isn't a heavenly kingdom where all are equal, where the lion and the lamb, the famous and the obscure, lie down peacefully together. That's only the pretense. It's not even true that we're treated alike: HHW and Teddy have the best rooms, for instance, just as Gladys Brooks and Virgil Thomson did last year.

But most of all I resent Anna May. Kenneth, always generous to everyone, forgives her as one would a child. That's how one ought to think of it, I suppose; but all the same I can't bear the idea that she was downstairs drinking champagne while I had to sit on the stars like a housemaid in a nineteenth-century novel, along with some of the best writers in America. As if artists were really a sort of servant – very likely what Undine Moffat herself believed.

Then, as Sally remarked, one only *suspects* that some members of the audience came for social reasons and that chamber music means nothing to them. Whereas she *knows*, from talking to her, that this is the case with Anna May. She also doesn't read seriously, doesn't really look at pictures. It's not art she's interested, in, it seems – only artists.

And yet, since she's Caroline's heir, she will presumably one day inherit all Caroline's paintings, her library, her unique record collection. More than that: all the letters she's had from guests for over forty years, the unpublished manuscripts they've left here, the scores . . . What will she do with them? Why, sell them, of course, Leonard said – still unread.

July 4

I feel very bad: cross, hurt and ashamed of myself. Just now at breakfast I behaved – *at Illyria* – worse than I ever would at home.

Again it's Anna May's fault; at least, it wouldn't have happened if she hadn't been here. Kenneth and I were sitting at the table by the window, quietly finishing our coffee, when she came bouncing over; and then started giggling and pretending to be afraid to speak to him. But finally she got breathlessly around to the point.

ANNA MAY: You really promise you won't be mad? Because I just *have* to ask you something. You see, we're all going to the races in Saratoga Springs for the day, *everybody*'s coming, and I want you to come too. It's the Fourth of July, a national holiday, you know! And I'm sure you need a holiday, you've been working so hard. Why, gosh, I've hardly *spoken* to you all weekend. I've been scared to, perfectly *petrified* (giggles), but Aunt Caroline says I *must* get to know you, 'cause you're one of the most interesting people here, she says ...

Besides, if you come, there'll be *heaps* of room in your yummy car, and then Leonard can take whoever's left over, so they won't have to go in Gerry's dumb old beetle that's probably going to break down anyhow. Please?

It seemed so obvious that she wanted Kenneth mainly as a chauffeur, since he happens to have the most elegant car here (Roz's new convertible); just as she invited Gerry to escort her to the concert last night because he'd look well in evening clothes. And I was so sure Kenneth wouldn't want to go that I spoke up, as I thought helpfully, and gave an excuse for him.

JANET: Oh, I'm sorry; we can't come. We've been planning to go to the parade in Jerico this afternoon.

And I explained how we wanted to see the Independence Day celebration (as we did last year and I'd assumed we would again). When Kenneth brushed that off like a fly and without asking my opinion agreed to drive Anna May and her entourage to Saratoga, I was stunned. And the moment she'd gone I said so, very untactfully.

JANET: Don't you see she's just using you? She wants to go to the races in a fancy convertible, and you have one; that's all. You'll have to drive for about six hours, there and back, through the holiday traffic. And there'll be an impossible crowd when you get there. It'll be awful.
KENNETH: I think it sounds like fun. We've seen the parade, there's really no point in going again; and I've never been to Saratoga before.
JANET: And you've never made a fool of yourself running after Anna May before.
KENNETH: What? ... You know, Janet, you're welcome to come along.
JANET: No thank you. I wasn't invited.
KENNETH: Oh, of course you were. Don't be ridiculous. Anyhow, it's my car. I'm inviting you.
JANET: I don't want to go to Saratoga! I'm going to stay here and work.

Not that I think I should have gone; it's sure to be an unpleasant trip – hot, noisy, crowded. But I should have showed less offense, refused more quietly. Maybe no one else heard my words; but they all must have heard my tone, even Caroline; and seen me stand up – declaring in a shaky high voice that *I* was going to *work* – pile my dishes and napkin clumsily together, and leave the table.

Behind me, as I marched out of the room, I could hear Anna May's unmistakable shrilly musical laughter.

That Kenneth could so suddenly and coolly desert me, to go scrambling after her with the rest of them – I can't understand that. Of course, only a few days ago he did the same thing to another woman – though under very different and extenuating (?) circumstances. When he walked out on Roz.

KENNETH: Roz got in last night, this morning rather, at about three AM, and she was in no condition to drive a car. So I didn't bother to wake her.
JANET: You left her a note?
KENNETH: She knows where I am.

I keep imagining, as if I were writing a story about it, a living room in western New York which I've never seen. On a sofa with a crumpled chintz slipcover Rosalind Foster, a small plump woman about fifty-four whom I've only seen once, is lying in an alcoholic stupor. She opens her eyes halfway; then slowly sits up, with ratty dyed-blond hair, half-undone clothes and a splitting headache. She stares blearily around the room; then, very uncomfortably, she stands. 'Kenneth?' she calls.

No reply. She stumbles barefoot through the house, looking for her shoes and her husband and trying to remember what the hell happened the night before. Outside, the sun is shining brightly on the grass-edged drive, but Kenneth's car isn't there; and neither is hers. Presently she goes into the pink-tiled downstairs bathroom and is sick into the pink-tiled sink.

Wasn't it really rather cool, almost spiteful of Kenneth to go off like that in his wife's car at seven AM? Surely he could have waited a few hours; or taken the bus here, as I did. Or at least left Roz a note. Compared to what she's done, it's not much, perhaps – but it's more than my idea of what Kenneth, Kenneth the Real Person, would have done.

I couldn't work after breakfast; I hadn't even enough

self-control to stay in my room and read until they'd all gone, but went and watched the departure from the upstairs porch. Behind the screen, which broke everything into confetti-like bits of color and shade as in a photo enlargement, I saw the cars load and drive off. First Roz's white convertible, top down, looking like an expensive magazine advertisement. In the front seat, next to Kenneth (in his best summer jacket), was Anna May. With her huge round dark glasses and yellow silk scarf, she looked like a lemur with a toothache. Ricky and Gerry sat in back, and as Kenneth accelerated rather ostentatiously up the drive, the long ends of Anna May's scarf blew back into their faces. Behind, considerably shabbier, came Leonard and Sally in Leonard's old MG, with Charlie Baxter packed sideways into the luggage space behind. For protection from the sun, he had tied under his chin an oversized straw hat such as Mexican book ends wear.

I suppose I ought to be happy. It's another beautiful summer day, and I have Illyria almost to myself: gardens, woods, pool, libraries. Anna May and all those other silly people will be gone all afternoon and all evening. And the day after tomorrow she's going for good.

She's going, that's true. But she's taking away with her, as it were, nearly everyone at Illyria; leaving in their place monkeys and pigs. All my friends—all of Paula's Lovely People—have vanished; and so has Lovely Janet. Leaving behind what everyone, myself included, must recognize as a rather petty, selfish, unlovely middle-aged woman – not better than her Westford self, but worse.

And I have over two weeks more, fifteen days, at Illyria. I have to see these people, in front of whom I've been humiliated and behaved childishly, every day at breakfast and dinner; and in between times I have to sit in this room and try to write. I have to be polite to Caroline, and keep all the rules ...

The anecdote about Felix Ledger. When he arrived at Illyria for the first time, Paula met him at the Lodge as she does everyone, and took him around. She showed him what paths led to the studios and called his attention to the sign requesting him to route his morning walk in another direction. She pointed out the rose gardens, where guests are requested not to pick the flowers. Indoors, she showed him where he was to work and explained at what hours he would be allowed to use his typewriter; she told him when meals were served and cautioned him against being late for them. Pointing out the relevant notices posted about the Mansion, she warned him to observe quiet in the hallways before four PM and after eight PM, not to remove books from the library shelves without signing for them, to always use the ashtrays provided and to refrain from smoking in bed, to please wash out his sink and tub with the tub cloth and the can of Bab-O after each use, and to kindly vacate his room between nine and eleven AM on Tuesdays and Fridays so that the maids could clean it. She demonstrated how to open the windows and which windows not to open, and said she sincerely hoped he would find his stay at Illyria pleasant and productive.

Ledger thanked Paula politely. He shut his door, opened his suitcase, lifted out a pile of shirts, laid them on the bed, and looked at them for a while. Then he put the shirts back into the suitcase, took it in one hand and his typewriter case in the other, tiptoed down the back stairs, got into his car, and drove away from Illyria forever.

Of course, I'm under no compulsion to stay here either. I can't just sneak off like Felix Ledger; not if I ever want to come back. But I could make some excuse – invent some family crisis – and leave tomorrow morning. Or even this afternoon. Why not, really? If I'm not working, I've no reason – or even right – to stay at Illyria. I could say Clark was sick, or one of the children. Then I wouldn't have to see anyone here again.

And I don't know if I want to, either. When Kenneth gets back tonight, I think I'd rather be gone.

But will he (will anyone) believe my excuse? Or will

he think (that is, know) that I've left out of spite and shame, in the jealous hope that Now He'll Be sorry? ... Well, he ought to be sorry. But would he be? Really, would anyone care if I went?

Caroline Kent would, in a way. She doesn't like to have her guests arrive late or leave early; she prefers Illyria to be fully occupied. If she suspects that my excuse was false, she'd like it even less. To the point, perhaps, of moving me onto the waiting list. (If she hasn't already done so after the scene this morning.)

Clark wouldn't mind my coming home early, but he'd be puzzled and surprised. And how would I explain it? Should I tell him, too, some flimsy lie? Or should I admit that I ran away because I behaved badly at breakfast?

No. I have to stay out my time at Illyria.

Afternoon

I've just heard something upsetting, about Kenneth. I don't know whether to believe it, or denounce the sort of idle callousness that spreads such rumors. Or both. Perhaps if I weren't already angry at him I wouldn't even think of believing this. And if he hadn't gone to Saratoga, I would never have heard it.

Anyhow, after realizing that I am morally and socially imprisoned here for the next two weeks, I spent the rest of the morning miserably failing to work. I couldn't even type: the keys felt sticky and hot, I made mistakes in every line and kept putting my carbons in backward. At noon I took my lunch box and went out into the calm, sunlit, generous landscape. I'd decided I would walk in the woods and have lunch in the most beautiful, calm, etc., place in Illyria – on the stone bridge by the far lake.

It didn't work. The dry Victorian–Gothic pine woods, the green mosses and white wood violets, the white wax water lilies floating on the lake, the fat brown ducks dipping their heads among the lily pads, didn't work. Illyria was still a prison – a prison with pretty wallpaper, that was all. I kept imagining how Kenneth and Anna May and the rest of them were at that moment roaring along the highway toward Saratoga. Maybe they would have a traffic fatality. Or maybe they were already there, and I pictured that: the crowds in the stands, the horses led past . . . Or I kept hearing him say to Anna May, over and over again, 'There's no point in going to the parade with Janet, I've done that before,' or whatever it was he said. Or inviting me, in that insincere light tone, to come with them.

Growing on the path by the bridge was a big clump of those rare ferns that Kenneth discovered the other day. It was so large that I had to kick it aside with my foot to get past. Because I was annoyed, I stopped and kicked it again, harder. Then I jumped on it. I suddenly jumped up and down on the whole clump of Kenneth's very rare ferns, and stamped them into the ground. The fuzzy dark-red spores on the underside of the fronds were already ripe, so that when I was through it looked as if some green animal had been injured there and bled.

Then I sat down on the bridge and tried to eat a ham sandwich, but I was so choked with shame and self-pity I couldn't swallow. The bread and meat stuck in my throat like chewed lumps of cloth. So I decided I would give my lunch to the ducks. I tore up the rest of the sandwich and threw it out onto the water. The ducks saw this, and all three of them came floating over. With their waxy orange beaks, they nudged the bits of wet bread and ham and lettuce smeared with yellow mustard. But they decided none of it would do; they all swam off fastidiously. And I was left sitting at the edge of a famous natural beauty spot which I had just trampled and strewn with garbage.

The same thing again. I feel awful, so I do something awful and make it all worse. One has to realize (I started to change that to 'you,' but desisted. Why should I banish Wun from Illyria? He's about the only friend I have left here. I thought Kenneth was my friend, my best friend . . . This day last year, this same afternoon, we were in Jerico at the parade. Not a slick professional show like Saratoga; but very amateurish, small-town – the children with toy flags; local merchants' homemade floats; plump, excited 4-H Club beauties waving to their friends; the band playing with such concentration they sometimes missed step. Kenneth bought us Popsicles from a cart: his orange, and mine lime because he'd decided it went best with my blue dress, and he said, 'You know, Janet, sometimes I think we're the same person . . .')

I forget what it was Wun had to realize. Nothing nice, anyhow.

After I'd ruined the landscape, I walked around through the woods and back by way of the studios. I thought I might call on Teddy, but his door was shut and I could hear the piano going, so I didn't dare. What I ran into instead was Nick Donato, sitting out in front of his studio (the one Rosemarie had last summer) on a crate, drinking a can of beer. He was surrounded by debris: heaps of battered electrical equipment and dirty bottles and painted scrap metal. Another little oasis of ugliness like the one I had just created myself, I thought. (I hadn't expected to see him; I'd assumed he'd gone with the others, though I realize now he wasn't in either car.)

NICK: Hi.

JANET: Oh! Hello. I thought you'd gone to the races.

NICK: Me? Nah. I've got better things to do.

But Nick's debris was composed of his works of art and their raw material, and he doesn't think them ugly. If he's pleased with something, he even calls it 'beautiful' – in the slang sense of the word: meaning apt, gratifying, expressively right. And what most people would agree was beautiful in the ordinary sense just doesn't interest him; it's not 'real,' or at least not relevant.

NICK: Hell, I grew up on the East Side, didn't even *see* the country till I was twelve years old and they sent me to Fresh Air Camp. What a letdown.

JANET: You didn't like it?

NICK: Like it? Sure, I *liked* it all right. It wasn't real, that's all. It looked like the ads, only not so good. The ground was kind of a dull color and there were all these rocks and broken dead leaves around that you don't see in the pictures. Parts of it were pretty, sure. In a phony way, like this place. Pretty-pretty.

Outside his own field, Nick is really more or less illiterate. Talking to him about books or music or ideas or people is like talking to some foreigner who knows only a few words of your language. Everything has to be translated, slowly and loudly, into Basic English, and in the process it usually disappears. But when Nick begins to speak of art, though he's still not conventionally articulate, it's very different.

According to him, there's a whole new race of urban men for whom the natural world doesn't exist significantly, doesn't really mean anything, since they've seen so little of it. They know live flowers, for instance, only as flimsy, ephemeral things – pale petunias or yellowed geraniums wilting in a box on a city window sill, stunted and coated with soot – in pathetic contrast to the hard bright plastic flowers indoors. If 'real' means 'having a continued definite material existence,' the plastic wins hands down.

And when they do finally get to see the natural world, it's too late. Used to the simple primary colors and shapes of manufactured objects, they find nature dim, finicky, flawed and disappointing. (As when Bessie visited Niagara Falls – it reminded her of the pictures, only it was smaller.)

NICK: An old-type painter like Kenneth Foster, probably he grew up in the country – it's what his work is about. For me these colors – all these greens, this diffuse light – And these shapes, leaves and stuff – they don't mean a damn thing, they just get in my way. Soon as I got here I felt smothered.
JANET: I know. When one can't work, however beautiful your surroundings are, it's like a prison.

NICK: Like a prison anyhow, this place. Got guards, bars, rules … Listen, when I took a look at that room they gave me, I nearly turned around and walked out. All those little tables and campy sepia photos and colored glass, Christ … This whole place is full of old crap.

Actually, he's got almost the nicest room in the Mansion – the one over the portico that Ed Loomis had last year, with the fireplace and oak paneling and big antique brass bed. But he hates it, and lives in his studio as much as he can.

It also embarrasses Nick to be waited on by the maids; Caroline's social manner makes him uncomfortable; and he doesn't care for the food: it's all too bland, and he can't have either wine or beer with dinner. He also complained that he's always hungry (possibly because his work involves more real physical labor than anyone else's) and said he'd been reprimanded by Caroline in writing for taking leftovers out of other people's lunch boxes. (At least, he thought they were leftovers.)

He's wanted to leave Illyria right from the start. But his house in Brooklyn is rented for the summer, his wife and children staying with relatives, and he has trucked all his equipment – welding machinery, tanks of fuel, a lathe, pounds of metal and wire and paint – up here at considerable expense. Even so, he plans 'to cut out as soon as I can swing it financially. This place is killing me.'

Considering the language barrier, we were getting on fairly well. I was thinking that whatever Wun might say against Illyria, it does have the advantage of exposing you to people you would never meet – much less really talk to – outside. (If you did meet them, there wouldn't be time to get beyond the stereotype.) And that Kenneth is wrong about the new artists. Some of them may be cynics and profiteers, but Nick's obviously sincere. Only, Kenneth doesn't realize that, because he and Nick never speak to each other – which is ridiculous, I thought; they ought to. ('Janet wants everybody to get on nicely in school . . .')

I tried to say this to Nick, to explain Kenneth to him, but what happened instead was that he started explaining Kenneth to me, in an awful way.

It was my fault, really. I know perfectly well that one should never discuss one's friends with strangers. I suppose I really wanted to hear him criticized, though I didn't quite want to do it myself. I wanted Nick to do it for me, and then I could defend Kenneth and feel loyal and virtuous. ('He hurt me, but I'm returning good for evil.')

JANET: I hope you don't think anyone who doesn't paint soda-pop bottles and stripes is through artistically.

NICK: I don't think he's through; shit, you can't say that about anybody as good as Foster. I just said he hasn't done much lately.

JANET: He doesn't have as much chance to work as you do. He teaches full time.

NICK: So do a lot of guys.

JANET: And besides, he has other problems . . . At home.

NICK: Yeah, I heard about it. His wife's a lush and she screws around. But all right, so what, he –

JANET: Who told you that?

NICK: A friend of mine, he was up there last fall, and she . . . Hell, everybody knows it.

JANET: Everybody knows it? . . . That's horrible.

NICK: What's the matter? You didn't know?

JANET: Yes, I knew, but . . . I didn't think anyone else did. Horrible. I can't understand it.

NICK: Huh?

JANET: I mean, I can't understand any woman's behaving like that, making herself a public scandal . . .

NICK: You think she should shut up and take it, huh?

JANET: Take it? What do you mean? Take what?

NICK: Being married to a fag.

JANET: That's not true.

NICK: Aw, come on.

JANET: Or maybe it's what she says, his wife ... I suppose she might want to start a story like that, to excuse her own behavior. But it isn't so, and you shouldn't repeat it.

NICK: Shit, Janet. I'm not trying to put Foster down. I got nothing against queers.

When I insisted it wasn't true, Nick only grinned and asked me if I had evidence to the contrary. Since I didn't, he obviously didn't believe me. And I wouldn't believe him. So I left. Not histrionically at once, but soon enough to show I was offended, though not shocked.

But I am shocked.

I know it isn't true, because I know how Kenneth feels about me. Even if he doesn't say it, or do anything about it. Because in fact our friendship has always had all the emotional overtones of a love affair, all the paraphernalia: charged looks and smiles, silly-fond presents and cryptic comic telegrams, special mailing addresses, clandestine meetings in New York at obscure foreign restaurants. Here at Illyria it's not even clandestine, and I feel terribly wronged when he goes off for the day without me. Everything's there, except the sexual guilt. But does that prove it's not true? Or does it prove the opposite?

What if Nick is right?

If he's right, then either Kenneth has been silently and consciously misleading me for two years, or I have been silently and unconsciously misleading myself. All this time I've been assuming that I was wholly in his confidence, as he was in mine; believing, really, that he was restrained when we were alone together from doing and saying in reality what he did and said in my fantasies only by an admirably fastidious sense of the real right Jamesian thing.

Isn't it a much simpler explanation that he didn't want to anyhow? That all this time I was being systematically deceived, and emotionally exploited?

But Kenneth isn't like that. I know he's not.

Then how could he have let me go on being half in

love with him, and acting as if he were more than half in love with me? If what Nick said is true, why didn't he tell me? When he's said so often how glad he is that he can talk to me, that I always understand everything so well . . .

Suppose he thought I knew. That could be why. If he thought I knew all along, but was too sensitive ever to ask any questions or make obvious references. That would explain why he's always praised me for my discretion, tact, etc. – to an extent that's sometimes puzzled me. (My tact in contrast to Roz, I suppose I thought.)

And he's said other things besides. Two years ago when Ned Rorem was here, Kenneth kept remarking how beautiful he was and how much he would like to paint him, if he did portraits. He's said the same thing about Gerry. Also that Gerry should never have married, and often that he, Kenneth, shouldn't have married. (Married Roz, I always thought he meant.) He even told me, only the other day, that Roz had some justification for what she did, which I thought was positively bending backward to be charitable.

It's true, too, that many of his friends, the people he's introduced me to in New York, I know to be queer, either by reputation or appearance. I even remember remarking on this silently to myself, and deciding it was a mark against the New York art world, but one more example of Kenneth's own generosity and tolerance – that unlike Clark and most other men I've known, he had no prejudice against homosexuals.

I should have suspected. Maybe, to preserve my illusion, I unconsciously refused to suspect. I wanted to go on thinking that, as I sometimes put it to myself, We Both Knew what we felt for each other, and that some day Kenneth would declare, if not express, himself. Stupid, self-deceptive –

Do I believe it, then? I suppose I believe it. At least, I don't *not* believe it.

I've been stupid about Nick, too, in a similar way. It was silly and rude of me to have thought that I must freeze him out when he tried to be friendly, because Teddy had declared he was 'after' me. Which he obviously isn't and never was; it was only another of Teddy's giggly inventions. Nick's at least five years younger than I am, and it's probably never crossed his mind to think of me as an 'outlet.' I've behaved, in both cases, like one of those awful elderly contraltos in Gilbert and Sullivan, convinced against both evidence and probability that men are after her.

Another letter from Clark in the afternoon mail, enclosing notes from the children. All three of them complaining. Clarissa wants to go visit a friend in Boston alone on the bus; Clarkie broke his tennis racket at day camp (in a fit of temper, apparently) and wants us to buy him a new one. Clark told them both No, and now they're sulking. Also he's had one of his headaches for forty-eight hours and is planning to spend the weekend in bed 'as far as possible.'

I have an excuse to leave Illyria now, or what could count as an excuse. Caroline still wouldn't like it, but Clark would be pleased if I came home, though surprised. He would think it a little silly and impetuous of me, but agreeably feminine and maternal.

Clark wants me to be a woman, but not a writer. Whereas Kenneth wants me to be a writer, but not a woman.

Only I don't want to leave yet. I feel like that man in Clark's department at Westford Casualty, David Sax, who kept deploring the state of the nation and saying how he felt like emigrating to Canada; annoying them all terribly. Then, as Clark put it, God called his bluff: he was offered a job in Alberta (mean August temperature, fifty-eight degrees) and had to shut up.

I don't want to go home, where the July temperature is so mean. Besides, how can I leave here without seeing Kenneth again, without knowing?

Something awful has happened. I don't want to write it into my journal. I don't understand it, even. But I have to try.

How it began, if I could go over that ... well, it began perfectly ordinarily. There was dinner, only four of us and Caroline in the dining room, at her table. I was feeling quite normal : still upset about Kenneth and about my work, but determined not to brood over it, at least for the evening; to think of other things. Indeed, I had a fascinating new idea about Anna May during the meal.

The way it came to me was, Caroline was speaking of the dress Anna May wore last night – which it appears was a gift from her. An odd choice, I could only think, while Teddy exclaimed politely and said how pretty Anna May had looked in it. 'Yes,' Caroline replied, lifting her fork so that the soft ruffle of her sleeve fell back from the hard birdlike wrist. 'She grows prettier and prettier.' And I suddenly thought, Miss Havisham. Miss Havisham speaking of Estella. And the idea came to me that Caroline Kent, who rumor says was deceived in love years ago by one of the first guests at Illyria, had chosen and trained Anna May to carry out her revenge on all artists, writers and musicians. That it was not Anna May's own whim, but rather her *assignment* to charm the men at Illyria and 'break their hearts,' insofar as this could be done in one long weekend. (And that possibly this weekend was only a beginning, a sort of rehearsal for what she will eventually do.)

Meanwhile everyone went on talking about Anna May and about Saratoga, and Nick Donato proposed that we should all go and watch what he called 'my kind of racing' – at the stock-car track over in Dryden, fifteen miles away. He invited everyone, including Caroline – who was surprised/amused/flattered but refused; as did HHW, but Teddy and I accepted. It didn't sound very charming, but I thought that it would be something to do, something to see. An aspect of the Modern World. And at least I wouldn't be sulking alone in my room all evening, trying hopelessly to work and listening for Kenneth and the others to come home.

So after supper we set off in Nick's old pickup truck, which he's painted all over with wild op-art checks and circles. By this time I felt even better, quite pleased with myself – with my brave determination not to brood, my insight about Anna May, the evening's excursion. Suppose my friends at home could see me, I thought fatuously, going off to the automobile races in this amusing vehicle, with a Famous Composer and a Well-known Pop Artist. Oh yes, that is the sort of unconventional adventure that Janet Belle Smith often has.

As I'd expected, I didn't much like stock-car racing; still, I liked it better than I'd expected. It's a sport for adolescent boys, based on *Popular Mechanics* expertise and love of speed and noise. A rusty unpainted iron and wood grandstand, the strong hot smell of burning rubber and castor oil. Steaming arc lights mounted on poles around the half-mile asphalt track; in the center an oval of grass and packed dirt strewn with trucks and trailers and cars and men in T-shirts.

I was afraid at first that Teddy and I wouldn't pass in the crowd, which seemed to consist of every man and boy I've ever seen working in a garage, plus all their wives, girl friends, parents and children. (There were lots of children, up well past their bedtimes, and even babies.) We should have changed, I thought nervously; my white pleated silk dress from Bonwit's was all wrong, and Teddy's seersucker jacket and pink bow tie even worse. But nobody paid us any attention, except to move clumsily but good-naturedly aside as we climbed the stand. Of course we were with Nick, who – in jeans, yellow T-shirt and black leather boots – was a natural. Actually, he looks lots better when he isn't dressed as he thinks appropriate for dinner at Illyria, in that awful shiny Dacron suit.

Even from the top tier of seats, the noise was dreadful. The explosions of the unmuffled motors breaking wind, the screaming tires, were unbelievable, even when one covered one's ears. And whenever they stopped for a moment, the loudspeakers overhead blared out popular music and local ads and announcements ('All right, boys! Let's have them cars for the third heat out on the track!')

The automobiles weren't streamlined or elegant at all; instead they looked like the ones in old comic books or Disney cartoons. They had open engines sprouting bunches of shiny exhaust pipes, and huge soft treadless tires (for traction). They were enameled glaring red, orange, green and yellow, with big black or white numbers on the side, and advertising slogans ('Dave's Used Auto Parts, Varna') or personal mottos ('Here Comes Crazy Jerry Wells').

At first I kept worrying that the drivers would hurt themselves, though Nick assured us that serious injuries are rare because the cars are so heavily reinforced. And in fact no one was hurt, but there were a lot of near misses and some awful-looking crashes, with terrifying sound effects and screams from the audience. One car went up off the track on the far side at about eighty miles an hour, and over the hill out of sight; but a moment or two later the driver, unharmed, was standing up in the white glare of the arc lights and waving his helmet at the crowd.

Gradually I stopped holding my breath and nose and ears and began to enjoy the spectacle, even cheering for the cars from Jerico and other nearby towns. And really, if one didn't care for tradition and had no aesthetic sensibility, stock-car racing would have much to recommend it. It's possible to see why Nick prefers it to horse racing. There's something nice about people cheering, as they were tonight, for their friends and townsmen rather than for their own hope of gain (there's no betting at auto races). And in spite of the picturesque elegance and brilliance of a place like Saratoga, there is something uncomfortable about it. I always feel sorry for the horses – so thin and nervous and specialized, ridden so hard by such thin, nervous, specialized little men. It seems proper that a machine should be created to run as fast as possible in a closed circle, but not an animal. Or a human being; there's something spidery, pathetic and repellent about most jockeys. The drivers tonight were tough-looking grown men who had built and owned their cars, instead of being hired by some rich fancier of horseflesh.

So despite the noise and smell and crude ugliness of it all, I rather liked being there, or at least the idea of being there. I liked sitting in the grandstand, drinking beer out of a cold dripping can with Teddy Berg and Nick Donato, noting their different responses. Teddy heard at least as much as he saw: he kept commenting on the overamplified rock 'n' roll, the various interesting (to him) auditory effects of the motors. Nick, by contrast, had all his attention fixed upon the visual spectacle; or on technical matters which he couldn't explain to us, since I don't know one automobile from another, and Teddy can't even drive.

The ride home was pleasant. All of us a little high on beer; Teddy encouraging Nick to tell stories of his childhood. His eccentric immigrant grandparents; the family's alternate feasts and famine whenever his father got work or was laid off; misunderstandings with welfare officials; the comic expedients by which they and the neighbors outwitted landlords and creditors. There were only a couple of times when another note sounded. Once when Nick told us that rats used to get inside his lunch bag and eat his sandwich before he got to school. We laughed too much, and he said it seemed funny to us because we didn't really believe him. (True, I suppose.) And again when he was talking about his 'rich uncle' in Mamaroneck, who owns a dry-cleaning business and has defrauded his customers and the income-tax bureau for years. This time we didn't laugh enough. We believed him, but the peculations of small Italian businessmen lack charm.

Whereas Nick's own background is strange enough to have seemed romantic to me? Did I imagine it as a sort of urban pastoral, scenes from *The Beggar's Opera*? And myself as one of those eighteenth-century ladies who pretended to be dairymaids and went tripping in costume among the cowpies? It wasn't quite that bad, surely; but maybe somehow – Oh God, I don't know.

Anyhow, the ride home was pleasant: cheerful, innocent – certainly innocent. And so when we got back to Illyria and it was still not dark, and the others not yet home, and Nick invited us to his studio for a drink, I accepted without thinking, or waiting to see what Teddy would do. And when Teddy said he had a rock-'n'-roll headache and was going to bed, I didn't think anything of it.

Nick's place rather startled me. One would never recognize Rosemarie's pretty studio – it looks like a small machine shop now. Nick's arranged it so that Illyria is completely shut out: except for the skylight, the windows have all been blocked up with shirt cardboards or flattened-out corrugated cartons stuck to the frames with black electricians' tape. There are sheets and strips of shiny metal leaning against the walls, piles of bent coat hangers and coils of wire, all kinds of heavy tools. Oily rags and cans of house paint; Coke cartons and beer bottles and old newspapers stacked in heaps. Colored advertisements and working drawings on graph paper are tacked up everywhere, and there's even a nude girlie calendar.

The first thing Nick did was to turn on his radio and locate the same sort of loud, mindless music we'd heard at the race track. Next he set out on a broken packing crate in front of the daybed a tin tray of ice, a bottle of bourbon and two smeared-looking glasses. (When I involuntarily commented, he rinsed them out in his dirty sink, without improving them noticeably.) I still thought I was collecting an interesting anecdote, and overlooked these sordid details – or rather I looked them over, in case they should come in handy when telling the story later, or writing about it.

Talking was impossible at first; one had to shout to be heard at all over the radio. But after I'd asked Nick to turn it down, it became easier – too easy even. Probably it was the whiskey on top of all those beers, but I found myself telling him how much I deplored the effect Anna May seemed to be having on Illyria, in fact how much I deplored her. I was happy to find he agreed.

NICK: She's nothing special. Just a dumb spoiled little bitch who doesn't know what she wants.

He described how she had come to his studio to pose, and gushed over a bentwood chair with two empty beer cans on it and one of his shirts hanging over the back, which she mistook for a work of art. (Not that that's such an unlikely mistake, these days.)

I liked his drawing of her too: he'd turned her into a kind of schematic, heavily shadowed Wrigley's Chewing Gum figure, all white teeth, orange tan and red bikini. He plans to execute it life size in painted metal and plastic, with real light bulbs that blink off and on.

According to Nick, Anna May deliberately encouraged him, and then scornfully turned him down 'in her high-society voice.' (She has no such voice really; it's merely middle-class suburban.)

NICK: She started to pose, but she got bored pretty soon because I wouldn't talk to her while I was working. So she took a break and walked around the place looking at my stuff, and told me what a great artist I was. Then she came around and gawked at my drawing, and complained about it in a kind of baby way, and let me feel her up for a while. I thought it was going to be easy. But when I started to peel that red bikini down off her ass, she put on her high-society voice and asked me what I thought I was doing, and who did I think I was? I didn't pay any attention, I thought she was just kidding. So then she hauled off and hit me in the face. Wow.

I sympathized, and began telling him the different

interpretations of Anna May's behavior that people have suggested, plus the one that occurred to me at dinner.

But since Nick had never read *Great Expectations*, I had to tell him the whole story, and even then he didn't understand. The idea that Caroline Kent 'wanted to get back at some dead artist who did her dirt over thirty years ago by making trouble for other artists and writers who maybe weren't even born then' seemed to him completely crazy. He was willing to believe it might be true; but if it were true, then Caroline was literally insane. Nor could he entertain the possibility of Anna May's being the (at least partly) innocent agent of retribution. ('Hell, Mrs Kent couldn't make her act like that if she didn't want to.')

Nick assumed, moreover, that I thought Caroline had got this peculiar scheme of revenge from Dickens' novel as one gets instructions out of a repair manual; and when I said I didn't mean that, he looked more puzzled than ever. The discovery of unconscious parallels between life and literature, which so excites me, is meaningless to him. The idea that Caroline herself might be only half-conscious of what she was doing was equally implausible. ('How do you mean? Either she knows it or she doesn't ... I don't get it.') Art is the only complex thing in his world; he sees everything else in abysmally simple terms. News is good or bad, tunes on the radio are great or lousy, people are good guys or bad guys.

And I saw again that though I didn't dislike him, I couldn't really talk to Nick and never would be able to; and I got up to leave – rather unsteadily. He said it was still early, offered me another drink, but I declined. I wanted to get back to the Mansion and see if Kenneth had come in.

I didn't think anything of it, or not much, when as we stood just outside the door Nick put his hand on my shoulder. '... And thank you again for taking us to the races ...' I think I was saying, when without warning he tightened his hand, pulled me toward him and said, 'Hey, Janet. I want to make love to you.'

I drew back, gave a little laugh of surprise, and replied that he couldn't do that. I was startled, but not really annoyed. Amused, mostly, and even a little pleased that he should say this. It was the final touch to the anecdote I had been composing in my mind all evening; not a detail to be related to everyone, naturally – not to Clark, for instance. But to certain friends, in the right tone of light amusement ... The tone I tried to take with Nick, in fact.

NICK: No? Why not?

JANET: Well, it's just not the sort of thing I do, you know. I'm a respectable housewife.

NICK: You are?

His response was to be a little incredulous, then a little hurt. (I imagine that in his own world he isn't often refused; and now, twice in two days—) I found myself assuring him as we stood there in the near dark that it was nothing personal; that there were, as he put it, no hard feelings; but that I really had to get back now. 'Well, kiss me goodnight, anyhow, huh?' he said.

And, being a little high, I thought that I might as well; that it would be polite; perhaps that it would improve my story. And possibly I also really wanted to.

And so I kissed him – and I couldn't stop. That's how it was.

It wasn't that I was forced, either. Nick, I suppose because of the work he does, is stronger than anyone I've known, but he kept it back at first. He kissed very gently, experimentally, and held me very lightly, so that it seemed impossible he still intended anything serious. But I do remember I noticed when we knelt facing each other on the daybed (somehow we'd got inside again and half across the dark room and onto the daybed), and he put one hand under each of my arms, pulling me up and toward him; for the first time I felt a tension, almost a vibration, in each hand, as of force restrained by greater force.

I did try to stop, though – several times. Once when he first reached inside my dress and I felt his fingers warm on my skin; and again later when he began to pull off my underpants. I gave another little yelp: 'Please! You mustn't do that!' I think I yelped.

Nick drew back from me at once and remarked flatly, 'So you're a tease too.'

I couldn't see his face in the dark, but there was so much bitterness in his voice, so much sour resignation (the slum child who's not really surprised when something is shown to him and then withdrawn), that I couldn't bear it. And I suppose I couldn't bear, either, being lumped with Anna May Mundy. And so I said, 'No, I'm not.'

The worst moment was when I'd finally taken everything off and Nick said suddenly, 'I want to look at you.' And before I could stop him he reached over me and turned on the light. The bulb glared out naked, and I grabbed for my clothes. I was abashed to expose all that soft, used forty-two-year-old flesh, creased in the corners like a pillowcase at the end of the week, and marked under the skin of the stomach and breasts with the irregular pale stretch marks of two pregnancies. I gave a cry and held my white dress to me, its sleeves dangling foolishly.

NICK: What's the matter? Come on. Put that thing down.
JANET: Don't look at me. I'm ... too old. I feel ridiculous.
NICK: Oh, shut up.

He pulled the dress out of my hands and looked at me, I think with pleasure, for a long while. And then I looked at him, and was frightened again, because he was so large. But not only frightened. Because when finally he put out one hand and touched the hair between my legs and said, 'You want to make it with me now, don't you?' I said, 'Yes.'

Then it was a long time later, a completely different time. It was as if I'd turned into a different person too –

or rather as if I'd somehow been that person all along. Nick even said something like that, and I agreed.

NICK: Zimmern's opinion was you were one of those cold society-woman types, nothing doing there, he said, but I didn't think so. I said, 'Oh no, not that one. She might make out like she's too good to fuck, but I'll bet you she loves it.' Was I right?

JANET: Mm.

Partly, I suppose, I agreed because I thought that if he knew I'd not slept with anyone but Clark for ten years he would feel smug, responsible, appalled – or all three. But mostly because at the moment it seemed to be true: I really was a woman of easy virtue and little refinement. I didn't mind coarse words and jokes and gestures, even enjoyed them.

For instance, there was a puddle of what looked like egg white spilled on the daybed, and I laughed when Nick made a crack about how he'd been storing all that up for two weeks. I said what I thought it looked like, and he said too bad he didn't have any powdered colors to mix with it so he could paint a picture in tempera for me. Then he grinned and drew a couple of lines across me with the egg white, and signed his name below them, just as it appears on his drawings in the gallery downstairs: N. DONATO. It felt warm and faintly sticky, but dried soon and stiffened. And I didn't mind; I laughed; and when he pulled me up toward him again I was surprised, happy.

Afterward I even thought up a coarse joke myself: I asked him if he always signed everything he'd made. Nick thought this uproarious, and so did I at the time, whoever I was.

What finally broke my trance, like a cold wind through smoke, was almost literally that: the draft of cool night air from the transom over the studio door. Chilled, I reached for my clothes and began to dress. More slowly,

Nick sat up; he stretched and yawned openly like some big animal. He pulled on his jeans; then picked up his damp T-shirt, smelled it, threw it across the room into a corner, and lazily took another shirt off the back of a chair. An awful, vulgar sport shirt with wide short sleeves, made of shiny green material striped in red and metallic gilt. As he buttoned it up, I suddenly saw him again: I saw a dark, strong-featured, vulgarly dressed young man with heavy arms and hands. And this person, as he took a comb out of his pocket and began publicly to comb back his too-long, too-shiny black hair, grinned knowingly, showing too-large strong white teeth, and said to me, 'You know something? You're a great lay. For me, anyhow.'

I just stared. It was as if I'd fallen into a pit. Such a man can say such a thing to me now, to Janet Belle Smith, I thought; since now I've given him the right to say it.

'Really?' I replied from the pit in a faint voice. I stood up, looking around the room at the greasy tools, the empty Coke bottles, the girlie calendar.

'Yeah,' Nick said. 'I think maybe I'll stick around here awhile after all.' He came over to me and put one hand, with its blunt stained fingers and dirty nails, on the white silk over my left breast, squeezing it in a knowing, proprietary way. And I stood and let him do this thing, which I'd just given him the right to do.

NICK: Hey. What's the matter?
JANET: Nothing. I'm just awfully tired.

I contrived a smile, then a yawn, and said I'd better go. Nick wanted to walk back with me, but I got out of it by saying we'd better not be seen together – by the watchman, for instance – at that time of night.

So at last he shut the door behind me. I stood a moment in the dark; then as my eyes adjusted I stumbled, then ran – not down the path toward the Mansion, but the other way, into the woods. Branches and bushes slapped my face and arms; I scrambled over stones. The next thing

I remember, I was wailing under my breath against the rough bark of a tree. It made a sort of long thin hiccupping sound, like a broken tea kettle; and it reminded me of something else too. But of what?

Finally I remembered. It was Teddy Berg's story about the seduced, dishonored Woman in White who sometimes appears and wails at night in the woods behind the studios. Only now I was her – or her ghost.

July 5

Nine AM

Already a hot, humid morning. I didn't go down to breakfast; I couldn't face the faces. And already I'm exhausted, after a mostly sleepless night full of wild ideas. For hours I kept tossing and turning among them. At one moment I would be shoving my face into the clammy pillow so as not to cry aloud with shame; at the next, the voice of that woman who had appeared in Nick's studio would warmly remind me of something that happened there, or make some bawdy practical comment.

For instance, at one point, I think about three AM, I'd decided I was going to go upstairs to Kenneth's room, wake him and tell him everything. I'll forgive him, I thought, sobbing silently; and he'll forgive me, for the shameful things we've done. Because Kenneth must think what he does is shameful, or he wouldn't have avoided mentioning it for so long.

And I would have gone – I even got out of bed and started to – except that *she* suddenly asked me what I thought Kenneth would imagine I wanted of him if I came crying into his room in the middle of the night in my nightgown.

Then I thought of leaving Illyria again. Only this time I wasn't going to make a plausible excuse and then depart; no, I would just run away, right now. With the calm of hysteria, I planned how I was going to get up as soon as it was light (I set the alarm for five), pack all my things, and carry them down to the road and hide them in the shrubbery by the gate. Then I would somehow climb the wall and walk to Jerico (six miles) and find a taxi. Because after what's happened, I said to myself, it was my *duty* to leave Illyria. It wasn't only that I'd done something so vulgar and disgraceful, I'd done it *here* ... 'Ah, come on,' said my other self. 'You really think there's never been anything of that sort here? What about Lou and Amy last year? What about Arnie and Rose the year before?' ... Yes, I said, but I'm not like them ... 'Oh no?' she asked. 'You thought you weren't like them maybe, but look at you tonight, when –'

I won't look at anything, I cried. I'm not going to wait for the alarm; I'll get up and start packing now, and – 'Don't be stupid, honey,' she said. 'If you really do that, you'll be sorry for it the rest of your life. Nobody will ever know you made it with Nick, but *this* they'll all know. Caroline, Teddy, H. H. Waters, Leonard ...'

Which is true, of course. I can't run away; but still, even this morning, when I think of living through the next fortnight here with both Kenneth and Nick, I feel like a character in Sartre's underground hotel. Somehow, I don't understand how, in only one week, I and all the company of the elect here have turned into knaves and fools; and Illyria, my heavenly paradise, into a kind of existentialist hell.

The other thing I don't understand is that it was so hellishly good. That in a sudden encounter with someone I hardly know, have nothing in common with intellectually or socially, and can't even talk to, I should experience more pleasure than with anyone except – occasionally – Clark. I've always believed it took time, years even, for two people to 'make a satisfactory adjustment' as the women's magazines put it. That, I'd decided, was why things weren't so good before I was married. That's the reason I've always given myself for the fact that even when I was most profoundly in love with Edwin, I was still physically better pleased with Clark, whom at the time I didn't even *like*.

Kenneth knows about Edwin; but this is one thing I never told him. I usually don't even think of it. It doesn't fit the story of my life, in which Edwin was the love of my life, the most intelligent, sensitive, attractive man I ever knew. Renounced, finally and so painfully, for a bushelful of the most intelligent, sensitive and attractive reasons ... Suppose Edwin had also been, in this one respect, like Nick. Would I have given him up?

Maybe not.

The second time, when at the end he finally knelt back and pulled me up to him, smiling and spreading my legs, and drove into me with such force ...

I don't want to think of that. I mustn't think of it.

Later

I've seen Kenneth, and we've made up. It's all right – or I suppose as right as it can be now. Which isn't after all very right.

I was lying on the sofa trying to read this morning when he came in and began apologizing even before he'd shut the door. First for disturbing me at 'work,' next for not having come sooner, and finally for his excursion to Saratoga.

KENNETH: You were quite right, you know. I shouldn't have gone yesterday.

JANET: Didn't you have a good time?

KENNETH: No. Not really. None of us did.

JANET: You didn't like Saratoga?

KENNETH: Oh, well, of course. It's immensely picturesque, as you know. Wonderful nineteenth-century Victorian architecture, with wooden towers, and colored pennants blowing, and the crowd very fashionable. And of course the horses are magnificent creatures. When they bring them out and walk them under the elms before each race, it's like a Degas. But you could see everything there was to see in half an hour, and we had to stay all day. And it was hot and crowded; and much too expensive. I didn't really want to bet, I had no intention to, but I got involved, and lost money.

JANET: Oh, I'm sorry. Was it much?

KENNETH: No, well, about twenty dollars. The price of a good frame, or plane fare to New York.

Apparently everyone lost money, especially Charlie Baxter, who can afford it least of all.

KENNETH: Gerry claimed he could tell the winners by looking at them up close and judging their animal energy charge, or something of that sort; but the horses he picked kept coming in last. The rest of us weren't too successful either. Leonard bought an expensive pink tip sheet, but it didn't help him much. He bet on the favorites and barely broke even; I did almost as well for a while choosing them at random by their names. Ricky couldn't bet after he lost the first two races because he hadn't any more cash with him, and Sally wouldn't bet.

But Charlie knows something about horses, and he knew how to read the racing form. At first he was doing remarkably well – by the fifth race he'd made over forty dollars, and we were all elated. Even though we'd lost, ourselves, it seemed a kind of victory for our side, for art ... I don't know ... Anna May was as excited as a little girl. It was her first day at the races, and Charlie said she brought him luck. She was really rather marvelous. When the horses came by she stood up on her chair, holding onto our shoulders, cheering and waving her program. But then Charlie started losing badly. Sally and I tried to get him to quit, but nobody else seemed to notice, or care. Anna May only kept laughing and coaxing him on. 'You see, you just double your bet every time,' she kept saying, as if nobody'd ever said it before, 'and then we positively *can't* lose!' Well, I suppose she's never had to think seriously about money in her life.

In the end, Charlie lost everything he had. Over a

hundred dollars, plus fifty more he borrowed from Leonard before the last race and can't pay back now, it turns out. He's very low today.

Though what happened was obviously Anna May's fault, Kenneth won't see it. Whatever happens, she must be innocent because she's young and pretty. (Indeed, he called her beautiful, and has even agreed to let her pose for him, though he hasn't painted a human face or figure for about twenty years.)

I feel sorry for all of them, and very sorry for Charlie. The trouble with magic games of any sort, from croquet to horse racing, is the magic depression that comes over the players when they lose. And since the odds in most games are against the individual player, one loses more often than one wins. 'As in life,' Kenneth said.

KENNETH: But it's not the money; it's the wasted time I regret most. And not just on my own account. When you realize that five people, some of them very gifted, gave up a full day of their working lives so they could watch horses running around a track . . . I kept thinking of you, sitting here working quietly and virtuously away, while we were squandering our time, our money and our dignity.

JANET: I wasn't, though. I wasn't working very well; I was too cross.

KENNETH: I'm sorry.

JANET: And I don't know what got into me, I felt so strange and upset that I . . .

I tried to tell Kenneth about what happened yesterday, but I couldn't get started, somehow.

KENNETH: Of course you were. We'd been acting impossibly. I really think we've all been a little crazy these last few days.

JANET: Yes, so have I –

KENNETH: You? On the contrary, you've been an example

of sanity and proportion. You and Teddy and Harmonia.

JANET: But I haven't. I've behaved very badly.

KENNETH: Really? What did you do?

JANET: Well, I lost my temper at breakfast, and was very petty –

KENNETH: Dreadful.

JANET: Don't laugh at me. I was. I was shrill.

KENNETH: I'm not laughing. It's only that you're usually so civilized, you blame yourself for a moment's well-founded irritation, while the rest of us –

JANET: I'm not so civilized, not at all. After you left . . .

KENNETH: Yes?

JANET: I couldn't work all morning, really. I felt deserted and full of spite and hatefulness. At lunchtime I went out into the woods, and I couldn't even eat my sandwich. And I was so angry at you, and myself, and everything, that finally I . . .

KENNETH: Yes?

JANET: I can't tell you. It's too awful.

KENNETH: Of course you can tell me.

JANET: You see, what it was, I decided . . . I felt wronged, and so I rebounded into another wrong. I don't mean it was your fault, at all. But I think that sometimes, when one's behaved like a rather second-rate person, the way I did at breakfast, then in a kind of self-destructive shock one goes and does something *really* second-rate. Almost as if to prove it . . . I can't tell you.

KENNETH: Go on.

JANET: I was walking in the woods after lunch, back by the studios, you know, and I . . . ruined your ferns. You know those rare ferns you found the other day, out by the stone bridge? I kicked them, and I stamped on them.

KENNETH: Really?

JANET: What do you mean, really?

KENNETH: Oh, Janet. Don't look like that.

JANET: But you're laughing at me again.

116

KENNETH: My dear, I'm not laughing at you; I'm laughing at both of us. I love you.

I meant to tell him; I began to, even. Then I realized what it was I had to say, what it would mean to him.

It's not only that Kenneth wouldn't like the idea of my having an affair. I remember he didn't much like it when I told him about Edwin, though that was long ago. But he would really hate my having it now, in this sacred place ('It's one of the best things about Illyria that there's so little of *that* here'); and above all, with this man. He might forgive, at least partly, my getting involved with anyone else: with Leonard, or Charlie, say. But that I should have anything to do with Nick Donato, the representative of everything Kenneth despises socially and believes is destroying him professionally, is unthinkable. It would seem like malicious, deliberate disloyalty on my part – both artistic and emotional betrayal.

And there's something even worse. If Kenneth knew what I had done last night – going out to a vulgar public place of entertainment, drinking too much and ending up in bed with a man years younger than I whom I hardly know ... What it would mean to him – what it does mean, I suppose, even to me – is that I have done and been exactly like Roz Foster.

So I couldn't say it. I only said how I'd been angry and destroyed his beautiful rare ferns. And Kenneth laughed and said what I've wanted him to say for two years: that he loved me. But it wasn't any good, because the beautiful rare Janet he thinks he loves doesn't exist any more, not since yesterday.

A sad idea just came to me: that Kenneth must have loved Roz once. He must have said so to her; maybe in the same way, in the same tone. Years ago, of course, when she was someone he could love.

And then another thought, an awful one. What if Roz is in love with Kenneth still (as presumably she was once)? Because otherwise why hasn't she ever left him? Since there were no children. Oh, but she isn't, I thought at first, or she wouldn't act as she does. But how do I know? Look at last night. Maybe if I were married to Kenneth I would do things like that all the time; and presently I would turn into Roz.

When Kenneth said he loved me, he smiled so warmly, and reached out as if he were going to touch first my face, then my bare shoulder, then my hand. But his hand shied at each point, quickly and vaguely stroked the air an inch or so away, and finally fell to his side again. Which is a good thing, really, I suppose, because if he had touched me or kissed me, I probably would have begun crying and told him everything. And he wouldn't have liked that.

He didn't really like it much about the ferns, but then he considered and said that they would come up again. I hope so. And I hope I will come up again.

There was a note in my lunch box from Nick, on the torn half of a sheet of cheap oatmeal-colored drawing paper. 'Can you come around to the studio for a drink at five?' it said. Of course I'm not going.

Afternoon

I feel a little, very little, better. The weather's still stiflingly hot, but I had a nice letter from Hortense saying New York is worse (102 degrees yesterday) and she wished they were here. I wish they were, too – then maybe none of this would have happened.

In a way, though, I feel it didn't. The whole thing was so unlikely, so incongruous. In a story one would never admit such a discordant episode – or even such a character as Nick Donato – into Illyria. And Nick *isn't* 'at Illyria' in any important sense. When he's in his studio, which is most of the time, he is obviously in New York City; and when he leaves his studio he's in some dismal rural spot of which it's correct to say (as he did when speaking of Roethke's breakdown here several years ago), 'Three months in this place would drive anyone off his nut.'

And when I went to Nick's studio, what happened was that I stepped out of Illyria into his world, and behaved like a character from that world, not like myself.

I'm glad I didn't tell Kenneth. First, because he would have taken it so personally. He would have made the connection with Roz, and thought I meant to accuse him – accused himself. (*Look what you drive women to.*) Which may be true, but if so it's not something he can change.

Besides, to expatiate upon this sort of momentary aberration is to give it more importance than it deserves. One has to avoid making much of an incident simply because it doesn't match the rest of one's life – when one ought for that very reason to give it less weight. The thing was an accident, the result of my strange emotional state at the time. I literally wasn't myself, but an emotional vacuum into which was projected the kind of person Nick wanted me to be. The fact is, it really wasn't I who went to his studio, but just some anonymous, lonely, half-hysterical woman in white, like Teddy's ghost.

Idea for story. Woman finds herself repeating cries and gestures of ghost in tale she has previously heard. Possibly in haunted house after she has waited (all night – all year?) in vain. Might be new tenant at first rather thrilled at owning a ghost (tradition, history, snob value, like genuine original paneling). Disappointed when it doesn't appear, feels cheated by real estate agent. Then something happens. A visitor – a repairman – Or maybe a telegram arrives. (Legend might be of woman who wails with grief at learning her husband is dead.) At end, she asks herself: But was she my ghost, or am I hers? Past and future time as possibly interchangeable.

I'm a little surprised that I should think so soon of using this material. But then I remembered Charlie's story.

He was having a terrible final quarrel with his wife, in which they were both crying and shouting and breaking things, and he had just in uncontrollable frustration thrown his cup of breakfast coffee across the room. And right in the midst of it a small voice within him remarked that it was important to notice exactly how the coffee cup looked striking the opposite wall, and to remember what they both did and said as it struck – more important than anything else.

After supper

A very hot, sticky evening. Roast lamb and blueberry pie for dinner, but nobody could bear to eat, at least at our table.

I told Leonard and Gerry (who are both now more or less cured of Anna May) my *Great Expectations* theory, which – unlike Nick – they grasped instantly and sympathetically, without insisting I meant it literally. Leonard thinks, though, that it applies mainly to Caroline – that if Anna May is supposed to 'break their hearts' she doesn't know it; that she's unconscious of the damage she does.

It's true, I admit, that she seemed quite unaware of the state Charlie was in at dinner. As soon as he came into the room (very late) it was obvious to most of us that he was drunk – his long pale face flushed an unnatural red, his voice loud and incoherent. He sat down heavily at our table and almost at once began to declare that his novel is crap and ought to be torn up, if he had any guts. He also made blurrily exaggerated self-destructive remarks about his own character, his debts and Anna May's refusal to have lunch with him. Possibly he was trying to get her attention, but he didn't succeed. She went on laughing and talking to Kenneth at the other table.

Instead, he got Caroline's attention (not unexpected, considering her eagle eye – but unfortunate, since Charlie

is more dependent on her continued good will than anyone else here). Caroline solved the problem with almost
frightening calm and dispatch: I saw her lean over and
speak quietly to Teddy, who got up and came over to our
table, where he spoke quietly to Leonard. Then the two
of them discreetly but firmly helped Charlie out of the
dining room. (Once they got him upstairs to his room,
apparently, he passed out at once on the bed.)

Even *this* Anna May didn't notice. Or pretended not
to; I would prefer to believe this, but I may be unfair.
I want to think the worst of Anna May because I don't
like her. I hate her, in fact; and I blame her for last night,
because if she hadn't come to Illyria it probably wouldn't
have happened. Which is worse than unfair; it's almost
crazy. But that's how I feel.

Actually I suppose it seems perfectly natural to Anna
May to lose interest in – even consciousness of – Charlie
Baxter, as soon as things begin to go wrong for him. It's
nothing *personal*. Only it wouldn't do any good to tell
him so, because he's determined to take her personally.
The fact that she gave back the manuscript of his novel
without reading more than a page or two proves to him
that it's no good – though Leonard, who read it all, thinks
the opposite. Leonard is an intelligent man and an important critic; but somehow, for Charlie, Anna May's
approval has become more significant.

And it isn't only Charlie. We were talking about it
after Leonard came back to the table, trying to figure out
what made everybody here fall in love with Anna May.
What quality could she possibly have that would attract
all these extremely different men?

GERRY: Listen, I can tell you that. Anna May has no
  qualities. She's a blank. Except for that intense attention she can turn on; that absolute agreement it looks
  like she's giving you, just because she's a blank. Like
  a mirror. You see in her whatever you want to see.
JANET: And what did you see in her?

GERRY: I d'know. Some idea of myself.

But of course the image in the mirror doesn't last. Anna May can't keep her attention fixed: it turns to the light, wherever that is at the moment. For instance, yesterday: on the way to Saratoga, and at lunch, Leonard says, she was concentrating on Kenneth and Gerry. But when they got to the races, they began losing money, so they looked dim in the mirror. As soon as Charlie started winning, Anna May transferred her attention to him, and hardly spoke to the others any more except to make fun of them.

Leonard thinks now that this shifting admiration has nothing to do with artistic talent, or even with specifically artistic success. Actually, he believes, Anna May's more blasé about artists than most people – even bored by them.

LEONARD: After all, a girl who sat on Virgil Thomson's lap at the age of three, and had nursery rhymes written for her by Robert Frost, isn't going to be much impressed with any of us.

Her attentions turns to success of *any* sort, no matter how trivial.

Anna May has invited everyone to Caroline's house this evening for a farewell party. But I'm not going. I want to start the new ghost story; also, I don't want to attend any party given and dominated by Anna May. I'm surprised everyone else does, after how she's treated some of them.

Even Nick is going. He came up after dinner, incidentally, and said he was sorry I hadn't been over for a drink. Then he told me to come around later this evening, 'any time after ten.' This wasn't even put in the polite interrogative mood, simply as a command. I replied as neutrally as I could that I didn't think I could make it. 'Well, you try,' he said, grinning.

Of course I'm not going. I hope this time he'll get the message, and I won't have to be rude.

I've just spent two hours on the haunted-house story, trying to persuade myself that there's some point in writing
it; which there isn't. There was something in the original
ideas, but then I changed the people to types, and the
precipitating incident from a seduction to news of a
death. Which is of course more conventional for a ghost
story, less apt to surprise or offend anyone – and also
isn't what I want to write about. I'm tired of ghosts –
whether they're real 'spirits' or just spiritualized versions of
myself and the people I know. I want to write about 'how
we saw the truck go by, and what it looked like and what
he said and what I said and what we thought about it.'

Really, I want to write all the stories I've thought of
and then discarded because they might shock or hurt
someone – about Illyria and about Paula; about insurance
men and Westford Casualty; and about my family.

Only of course I can't.

I smiled and inwardly demurred when Gerry said I had
a patron, as writers did in the seventeenth and eighteenth
centuries. But it's true. Clark and all the rest of them are
my patrons just as much as those English lords were
Dryden's or Pope's. And my writing shows this depend-
ence exactly as theirs did. There is the same avoidance of
all topics which might annoy them; the same gross or
subtle glorification of their way of life; the same praise
of their virtues (reliability, good taste, justice, modera-
tion) and blindness to their faults.

Hopeless. The whole thing is hopeless.

I just went down to the kitchen to make myself some
iced coffee, and found H. H. Waters there boiling water
for tea. (Being from the Deep South, she finds this weather
quite normal, even reasonable.) I was so discouraged and
depressed that I found myself telling her how Clark was
my patron, and what that meant. Besides, like other shy

people I've known, she has a way of saying 'Yes?' and looking at you out of those huge bulging eyes that makes the most trivial remark turn serious. She nodded intently as she measured tea into the pot and said, 'There's a rule, I think. You get what you want in life, but not your second choice too.'

There was one man in her past, she confided, who would have married her if she had agreed to his conditions. It was a good match, suitable in every way:

HARMONIA: He didn't mind my being so plain, or my peculiar relatives, because they were his relatives too – he was my second cousin. The only thing Lee objected to was my 'poetry-writing.' He mentioned one evening, when we were walking in the yard under the grape arbor, that he took it for granted I was going to give all that nonsense up after we were married. I'd be too busy for it anyhow, with our social life and managing his place and the help, and of course later taking care of our children. He expected it would just kind of stop naturally, he said. But I said I didn't expect it would …
   Well, in the end, the wedding never came off.

I asked if she'd minded much. 'Yes,' she said, which surprised me – she'd told the story so lightly. 'I was in love with him, so I minded a deal at the time. But finally I said to myself, "Lee is short, and Art is long."' (And she gave a sad laugh.) 'Indeed, Lee *was* short—shorter than I in shoes.'

I don't think I could have done what she did – given that choice – when I was engaged. And now – Now that I have a family, and care what they feel, and what the world thinks of them …
   So either I have to leave Westford, which is impossible; or I have to go on writing stories that don't mean anything, which is stupid and boring and miserable.
   Or stop writing entirely.

July 6

A strange night. At eleven o'clock Kenneth still hadn't come back from Anna May's party. I felt so tired and baffled about everything that I went to bed. And then of course I couldn't get to sleep. It was very hot and close. There was a big fly buzzing around the room, and the fine sheet, damp with heat, weighed on me like a coarse blanket. Even my nightdress was too much, but when I took it off I felt annoying puffs of air from the open window, as if some large animal were outside, breathing up against the screen directly onto my skin.

Finally, after about an hour of this, I decided to go for a walk and see if I could cool off.

It was dark out, another heavy, starless night, silent except for those warm animal breaths of wind in the pine trees, and the crunch of my sandals on the gravel. Without thinking about it, I took my usual route along the drive past the garage and the studios, all dark now. Except for one. Though it was getting on for twelve, there was a light in Nick's studio.

I stopped short on the path, frowning. The idea that Nick was still waiting up in there, presumably for me, made me irritated, nervous and guilty. I thought to myself that I had behaved rather badly to him by his standards; and even by my own. That it was cowardly of me, and mean, to let him go on expecting I would come, and thinking of me as a possible outlet. That though I might not care for Nick, and might think he had exploited me in a moment of hysterical weakness, he didn't know that – because I hadn't let him know. Really, I owed him an explanation, and the sooner the better.

Therefore, at midnight, telling myself that the fair thing, the honest thing, was to explain to Nick Donato that I was never going to his studio again, I went to his studio.

And of course what happened was what anyone in his right mind would have known would happen.

So it wasn't just an accident, a momentary aberration I should try to forget; you can't say that of something which takes place twice running. Nobody forced me, either; I did it deliberately. Maybe I even went out for that walk deliberately.

And we'll both be here over two weeks more, so it can happen again. And again. It will happen again — I even want it to.

Another surprising thing was what occurred afterward. We were lying there on the daybed, and Nick was talking about his work, his plans for this fall — and all of a sudden I started crying, I suppose because I didn't have any plans for my own work except probably to give it up.

So of course he asked what was the matter, baby. I didn't want to tell him, or think it would do any good, but I couldn't help myself — it all came out, in a kind of damp confused hiccupping rush, interrupted only by my stopping from time to time to wipe my nose and eyes on a paint rag. About Clark, and the harm I had done him and the children by letting those stories be reprinted; and H. H. Waters and her engagement; and how I couldn't write any more and therefore didn't deserve to be here.

Nick didn't really understand most of this, but he said some interesting things. For instance, when I was telling him about Clark's dislike of my writing, contrasting it with his own situation.

JANET: Artists have it much easier. You'll never run into that sort of problem.

NICK: You must be kidding. You think my wife likes my work? Hell, no. Oh, she wouldn't say so to me, and she keeps quiet when other guys tell her how great I am, but down in her heart she thinks the things I'm making now are ugly and cheap-looking.

Anita was really happier when I was teaching. I didn't make much, but it was a steady job. Now that my stuff's started to sell she's in a bag. She likes having all that dough, but she's scared shitless it won't last. Every time I want to buy something she goes into a panic and starts talking about the kids' education. Like I wanted to rent this house on the beach for the summer – two thousand dollars. She thought I was crazy, when we could stay at her mother's place for nothing, if I could stand her mother.

His wife's middle-class parents both disapprove strongly of Nick's art, which they consider pornographic and un-American. When this country gets back on the Right track politically, people like him won't be allowed.

Nick's own family also thinks his success won't last, but to them it's all a big joke.

NICK: When I had my first show, my uncle Frank came in from Mamaroneck, a big honor for us. He couldn't believe it. He went around the gallery laughing his ass off. 'They pay you seven hundred fifty dollars for *that*?' he kept saying. 'They must be crazy.' Then he pulled me over to the window, and whispered, 'You got the cash?' 'I got a check,' I told him. 'Nah, you get the cash, Nicky,' he said. 'Right after we leave here, we go down to the bank. With people like that' – he was tapping his head, this way – 'you got to act fast, before they change their minds.'

'Lissen, that's nothing,' my father told him. 'You oughta go downtown, Frank, and see the place he's working now.' (I had a class at Cooper Union then.) 'Has he got a soft job! Nothing to do all day but walk around this big room and look at girls drawing pictures.'

What struck me was that Nick agrees with his father. He does really think he has a pretty soft job. It has never occurred to him to agonize over the pains of the creative life as so many of us tend to do.

I told him how Teddy Berg had advised me, apparently seriously, to leave my family and come to New York; I half thought he might agree. Instead he just laughed, groaned and shook his head. (By this time I'd stopped crying, and he had made us both another drink.)

NICK: Naw, that doesn't work. I tried it. When my pictures first started selling, I got a swelled head from all the publicity and invitations I was getting, and the expensive chicks who suddenly started looking available. The baby had the mumps, and Anita was giving me a hard time at home. So I thought, who needs it? I'm a big success now, I can have anything I want. So I rented this classy studio on Tenth Street, put in a kitchen and a double bed ...

It was no good. The first thing was, I couldn't work any more. In Brooklyn I had my studio up at the top of the house; it was quiet, and Anita answered the phone and kept away people I didn't want to see. A nice view, too; it was okay.

In Manhattan, on the other hand, Nick was interrupted all day long by visits and telephone calls. Dealers, critics, photographers, journalists, collectors. Friends of friends who wanted to buy a painting without the gallery markup, and girls who wanted one more or less for nothing.

NICK: And I mean nothing. Most of these New York chicks, they're not so interested in screwing as they look. Oh, they'd put out, all right, because that was part of the bargain, you know what I mean? But what they really wanted was to get to be Mrs Nick Donato, or if they couldn't make that, then they wanted to be seen around with me and have it known all over town that they were going with me ...

They didn't even listen when I talked to them. You take a girl like that Anna May to an opening or a party, she's always looking over your shoulder to see what reaction she's getting, or if somebody more important has just come in. And when you finally get her alone, she doesn't really want to fuck, she wants to complain and throw a scene.

It took him five or six months, Nick said, to realize that he'd had it.

NICK: I missed my kids – I was seeing them every weekend, but hell, I wanted to see them every day. And I missed Anita ...

Art International came out with an article on me, how I painted a picture and what a swell guy I was, with photographs, but it was all crap. I hadn't finished anything in weeks, and I was turning into a louse. So I moved back home.

I have no desire to live in New York; but I must admit I've had my own fantasies: a small house off Brattle Street (usually it is dark gray with white trim) where I can keep the cats Clark and Clary are allergic to; or perhaps a flat in London (Chelsea or Hampstead) in which I serve afternoon tea to friends I now know only from correspondence (my collection of old china has of course crossed the Atlantic intact).

In fact if I left Clark and the children I'd be even more miserable than Nick was. And so guilty. I'd have to spend most of my time in Cambridge or London explaining (aloud and in print) why I'd done this awful selfish thing, justifying myself ... In the end it would be terrible for my work too.

The most striking remark Nick made was when I told him I felt so hopeless I was thinking of giving up writing.

And he said, the way it sounded to him, that was what I'd already done. He didn't mean just the trouble I've had working here, or at home this spring. He meant that when I decided not to write stories that would embarrass Clark and the children, I gave up writing seriously.

Which I suppose is true. Not that it happened all at once. I censored myself gradually over the years – as the children learned to read, as Clark became more prominent locally, as my stories began to be published in magazines more people read.

I've said this already, of course. But what I see now is something else even more disquieting. It's that over the years I've begun to avoid doing – and sometimes even seeing – anything I couldn't write about. (Gerry Grass's mistake in reverse. He does things merely so he can write about them, which doesn't work either – because then he has the experience mechanically, without any real impulse toward it. I have the impulse, but usually I deny it, and also deny myself the experience.)

For instance, I wouldn't want to write about being in love with a homosexual for two years, so the simplest thing was not to notice that I was in love with Kenneth or that he was a homosexual. And I decided I would forget all about Nick; it hadn't really happened, I told myself, and anyhow he wasn't even here, and I was just a ghost.

It would be different, much easier, if I were the kind of writer who creates his own world: a serious historical novelist, for instance; or the author of Kafkaesque fantasies. Only I've never had that sort of imagination; my stories have always been close to real life, dependent on it for both subject and attitude.

But why can't I recognize and experience things, and then just choose not to write about some of them? I suppose because it isn't agreeable to know there are large areas of life you're afraid or ashamed to deal with. Everyone knows that writers who limit themselves in this way become trivial, repetitive and boring.

Trivial. Repetitive. Boring. What my stories have lately

become, in fact. As a result of living to suit my work, in an ever-contracting circle of experiences and perceptions.

Later

I just heard what else happened last night – Charlie Baxter had a drunken breakdown. I didn't know it before, because I didn't get up for breakfast, but when I went down for my lunch box I met Gerry, and the first thing he said was, 'Hey, I hear Charlie's much better.'

Apparently, some time after he passed out in his room yesterday evening, Charlie came to. Teddy and Leonard hadn't thought to take his liquor away, and so he started drinking again and brooding about Anna May and his novel. About midnight he decided to destroy the ms. So he tore up all the pages, crammed them into the wastebasket, and then set them on fire.

The first anybody knew about it was when Kenneth, across the hall, began to smell smoke. Charlie had locked himself in and he was too far gone by that time to open the door, or else he didn't want to. When Kenneth and Leonard and the night watchman finally broke into the room, Charlie was slumped half-upright on the sofa in a kind of stupor, and not only was the wastebasket burning but part of the carpet as well. They put the fire out with extinguishers, but it was a near thing.

I went over to the pool with Gerry to eat lunch. It was very hot, but cloudy – I didn't go in. Leonard, Teddy and Sally were already there, talking about Charlie.

They all had different reactions. Teddy took it very lightly, as if it were just another comic incident in the history of Illyria which had happened twelve months or even twelve years ago instead of twelve hours. Sally, like me, was upset – also worried that Caroline will now expel Charlie. But Teddy assured her that isn't likely.

TEDDY: She knows he's got no place else to go, for one thing. Anyhow, Caroline doesn't take what happened last night so veryvery seriously as you do. She's seen a lot worse than that in forty years here. Charlie didn't kill himself, after all, and he didn't do anyone else any harm – didn't even damage much furniture ...

You've got to remember, m'dear, Caroline doesn't live in the present moment the way most of us do. She takes the long view, you might say the historical view. And when you think in terms of twentieth-century American literature as a whole, C. Ryan Baxter is an important writer.

Leonard didn't care half so much about Illyria, or about Charlie, as he did about Charlie's manuscript. After the fire was out, and a doctor had come and given Charlie a shot and put him to bed, Leonard took the wastebasket to his own room to see what was left of the novel. All he found was a mess of soggy, charred pulp and ash. A severe disappointment, for which he blames the irresponsibility and egotism of artists in general, and Charlie in particular. It was just like Baxter, he remarked sourly, to keep no copy.

For Leonard it is a real tragedy that the book is gone (unless Charlie is able, and more important willing, to re-write it).

LEONARD: You don't take it seriously. None of you here really gives a damn for anyone's work but your own. And you never believed in Charlie anyhow – I know, nobody does any more. But I saw that manuscript ... As it's turned out, I'm probably going to be the only literate person in the world ever to have read it.

As he said this, Leonard smiled bitterly but also rather proudly.

I also think there's been a tragedy, but I blame it mainly on Anna May – though possibly she was only the precipitating cause. But I think that if Charlie gives up now, it will be as clear a case as I ever saw of an artist destroyed by the thoughtless fickleness of the world.

Gerry, on the other hand, considers the loss of the novel a good thing. The destruction of any established system or institution is good according to his philosophy; and since Charlie had been working on this book for over five years, it qualifies. Gerry thinks Charlie will rise phoenixlike from the wastebasket – or if he doesn't, it will be because he's still trying to do with booze and Marx what's better done with mescaline and Buddha.

I don't know what Kenneth thinks, because he didn't come to the pool for lunch. Sally says he was still making drawings of Anna May when she went by his studio, and seemed very absorbed. He must be, or he would have come around this morning to tell me what had happened.

On my way back I met H. H. Waters, who asked anxiously after Charlie. She told me that she thought 'something dreadful' was going on last night, but was afraid to find out what. She heard 'shouting and pounding and banging' upstairs and hid her head under the bedclothes, 'trying not to imagine horrors.' Even in the light of day she didn't really want to talk about it. And yet in other ways she's so brave – far braver than I. One reason she's been working so hard here, Teddy told me today, is that she has to have an operation this fall which may not be successful.

I don't want this to happen; I don't want H. H. Waters to stop writing, or Charlie either. And I don't want to stop writing myself. It wouldn't work, anyhow.

If I gave up my family I'd be not only miserably lonely for them, but in the end a worse writer. And if I gave up writing, I'd be a worse housewife. I might spend more time at it, but so much of that time would be devoted to self-justification, to silent or even noisy demands that my husband and children appreciate and reward the sacrifice I was constantly making for them ... It's awful to think of the sort of person I would become.

I've torn up the stupid ghost stories and started writing about Paula and Illyria. I can't publish this, of course, if

I ever want to come back here, but at least I can get it down on paper.

Evening

Two good things: it's finally rained – a heavy black thunderstorm this afternoon; and Anna May has left, in a red sports car with a red-faced Dartmouth student. Since this happened just before dinner when everyone was downstairs, it was a very public departure. I would suspect her of having timed it, except that she seemed so bored by the whole scene and by everyone who came out to say goodbye. She looked at us, as we stood around the car under the still-dripping trees, as if we were a pack of elderly cousins with whom she had *faute de mieux* associated for a few days, and couldn't wait to see the last of.

Charlie wasn't there to see Anna May off, but he came down to dinner, looking rather shaky but normal. He said he felt fine – and that he had no intention of writing his novel (or any novel) ever again. I hope this isn't true.

It was so warm, and the grass so wet, that nobody wanted to play croquet after supper. Instead we all walked over to the pool house (except for Ricky Potter and Sally Sachs; reunited by Anna May's departure, they'd gone off somewhere together). Teddy had brought white wine and soda for everyone, as a kind of farewell party for H. H. Waters, who is leaving early tomorrow. She apologized to us for 'having been such a hermit these last days' and explained that she'd been trying to finish a long poem. (While the rest of us were running around having emotions, she and Teddy went right on working.)

Some of us went swimming – including me, which proves that Anna May is really gone. And we drank wine and soda, and held a sort of post-mortem on her visit. The general conclusion was that she is, as Charlie put it, just someone who doesn't comprehend the arts and never will.

CHARLIE: There are a lot of people like that in the world, you know. They may learn to disguise it more or less, but essentially they're color blind, tone deaf and indifferent to the sound of words. They never once in their lives go to a museum or a concert to see or hear something, or buy a book because they really want to read it, though they may do it all the time for social or economic reasons.

It's pathetic for her as well as for us that she should be Caroline Kent's goddaughter.

We also decided that basically she's rather simple, even a little stupid perhaps – without any of the complex perceptions and motives we've all been attributing to her. The fallacy that beautiful people must be sensitive to beauty. (Synecdoche, Leonard said – confusing the container with the thing contained.)

Kenneth described how Anna May came to his studio to pose yesterday and looked at everything for a long while without making any comment. He thought by turns that she was too shy, too moved, too scornful to speak. But finally he realized that she was looking not *at* his paintings, but through them.

KENNETH: At last she remarked that there was a Mr Avery who always had that room when she was a little girl; and that she used to come and see him and he would always give her a Hershey bar. I puzzled over that one for half an hour. First I thought she was making a subtle, probably unfavorable comparison between my work and Milton Avery's. Then I told myself not to be paranoid; she was just making conversation. But if so, she didn't care to make more. I wondered if she wanted me to give her the adult equivalent of a Hershey bar, and if so what that would be. She didn't want wine or whiskey; she finally accepted instant coffee but didn't drink it, only smiled abstractedly and fidgeted with the cup. I suppose in her mind she was already far away from Illyria ... Later I asked her what Avery had been like. 'Who?' she said. 'Milton Avery,' I repeated. 'Oh,' she said. And then, after a long pause, as if for profound consideration, 'Nothing special. He was just an old man.'

The truth is, Anna May had literally no opinion of Milton Avery, or of Kenneth's paintings. And not just because she's young. As Leonard said, when she is fifty she'll still have no opinion.

But if Anna May is so simple, where did all our complex explanations of her come from? From within ourselves, obviously. Everyone interpreted her according to their own desires or fears. Leonard thought her an anti-Semite; Nick at first believed her an easy lay; Gerry said she cared only for fame and success, and Teddy that she was an innocent child.

My own ideas about Anna May varied with my mood from one day to the next. In the beginning, when I admired everyone here indiscriminately, I thought she did the same. When I discovered that some of them were weak, I postulated that she was a kind of artistic detective employed to reveal this weakness. And finally, after I had found out about Kenneth and was brooding over his concealed dislike of women, I thought Anna May the agent of Caroline's long-concealed dislike of men.

Of course there is no guarantee that all of us were wrong all the time; perhaps Anna May really is one of the figures we imagined, perhaps none – not even the ignorant coed Kenneth saw in his studio.

Meanwhile the real Anna May, whom we will never know, escapes in a red sports car.

But in the long run, it doesn't matter. Because, as Leonard said, some day Anna May will be fifty; some day she will have ceased to exist at all. Nothing will be left of her as she was this weekend, except for Nick's 'American Girl with Coke No. 3,' Charlie's novel (if he rewrites it), Gerry's poems, and the sketches Kenneth drew. Plus whatever the rest of us may make of her. Already these portraits don't agree (Nick's Anna May will have lemon-yellow plastic hair – Gerry calls it 'sunburned'). Like our explanations of her character and motives, they aren't the real Anna May, but her reflection in different distorting mirrors.

Yet the real Anna May Mundy will presently disappear, while the false versions are potentially immortal. 'Forever wilt thou love and she be fair.' What's more, 'she' will be fair not as she really was in life, but as 'thou' described her. In this sense, all the men here who didn't 'make' Anna May will have made her forever. They win; we win, in the end.

Art has the last word. The future and the past both belong to us. But how about the present? No. Jam yesterday, jam tomorrow, but never jam today.

July 7

Morning

Wrote more of the Illyria story. It's going to be good – too good not to publish. Possibly, someday – If Paula ever leaves Illyria – Or if Caroline decides not to ask me back – as she may if she hears what I've been doing lately. And I have to take into account that Caroline may hear of it. Because as soon as anyone not directly concerned in a secret finds out, it's not really safe; and now Leonard knows this one.

I suspected it yesterday evening. We were swimming, and Nick dived in and came up between my legs, much too close. I didn't want to protest and attract attention, but I paddled aside a stroke or two, took hold of the diving board to steady myself and looked around to see if anyone had noticed. It was dusk, but the pool is lit from below and I thought I saw Leonard, down at the other end, glance from Nick to me. I even thought I saw him smile knowingly at me as I hung from the board, with my hair tangled wet over my face and my legs floating pale and helpless in the transparent chlorine-green water. I wasn't sure, though, so for a while I forgot it.

But later in Nick's studio I remembered, and I asked Nick if he had said anything to Leonard. I expected he would laugh and tell me not to be so nervous. Instead he admitted it without much hesitation, or even apology.

NICK: Yeah. See, he asked me. (Shrugs) You don't mind?
JANET: Of course I mind! When you promised –

I suppose I should have known Nick would tell some-body, when he said for me not to worry about it that first night.

JANET: You won't tell anybody?
NICK: No, why should I?
JANET: I just thought –
NICK: Don't worry about it, baby.

'Don't worry about it' is what Clarkie and Clary always say when one should in fact worry. ('Are you wearing your boots?' 'Have you done your math homework?' 'Don't worry about it!') And why should I have expected any-thing else, after I've seen Nick play croquet, and noticed even that first evening that 'when he wins he shouts and grins and waves his mallet'?

I'm angry, really angry, so seldom that it always takes me by surprise. At first I think it's fever and chills, that I'm getting the flu or something; and when I realize what's happening, I don't know how to express it with the proper force. I felt it was undignified to be furious with nothing on, but I did the best I could: I stood up, partly shielding my nakedness with a red striped pillow, and told Nick he had been vulgar, dishonest and disloyal. He only laughed. I suppose I did look funny; it's also the differ-ence in our emotional style. What would seem cold, fatal fury in Westford only registers as annoyance on a Brook-lyn scale.

NICK: Aw, come on, Janet. What do you care if Zimmern knows? You think he's going to tell your husband or something?
JANET: No, it's not that . . .
NICK: Well, all right. So why all the flak?

I couldn't answer; I couldn't explain that though I was willing to go to bed with him, I was ashamed to have anyone know it. So I said something about Caroline not inviting people to Illyria to make out, and disapproving of guests who used the place that way. And maybe, I said, she was right. At this, Nick first became scornful, then softened. He got up, put his arm around my shoulders and tried to reassure me.

NICK: That's a lot of shit. Nobody's going to tell Mrs Kent anything. It's none of her business ...

Listen, baby, don't let her get you down. I know how she comes on, like this place belongs to her personally, and everybody has to act like they were at a tea party all the time, but you just got to ignore her ... Come on, let's lie down again ... Hell, what difference does it make what you do here in your spare time? Who gives a damn, long as your work is okay?

Of course this is true in a certain sense. Historically it doesn't much matter if Charlie gets drunk, or Leonard insults people, or I fall into bed with someone I hardly know. In the long run, we won't be judged by our private behavior, but by what we've written. Like Anna May, we will survive only through art, though differently.

That's what Charlie meant that night at the coffee house, when he said that all of us here were free, at least while we were here, to look and act as we liked. Because our economic function wasn't to *be* something, 'to perform some role in the capitalist world' – but to *make* something.

CHARLIE: One time when my wife was up here, Caroline introduced her to Robert Lowell out by the garage, and she didn't even stop to shake hands. 'Well, for Christ's sake!' she complained to me afterward. 'How was I to know? She just said "Mr Lowell." You see a man in jeans and a cruddy old shirt walking along the path with a tin lunch box, like a construction worker, what are you supposed to think? What does he want to look like that for?' 'Because he *is* a construction worker,' I told her. 'We all are.'

It's true; people at Illyria often do look like the sort of men who come to fix the washer, shingle the roof or blacktop the driveway. They have the same indifferent, absorbed manner – and/or lack of manners. They push ahead of you at dinner occasionally, interrupt and contradict you, don't even answer sometimes. But when they do answer, you know it's because they're interested – not merely being polite.

Teddy Berg said the same thing:

TEDDY: I had an old professor of harmony, used to quote Yeats to us all the time. 'You must choose perfection of the life or perfection of the work.' Well, the idea of a perfect life sounded terribly dull to me, even then ...

In Westford, I suppose, I am trying to live the perfect (Westford-perfect) life – to be a good wife and mother and do the right thing. And it's not like a story, which can be finished. The Right Thing has to be done over and over again every day, like any housework.

But for Illyria the perfect life is irrelevant. In the long run, it's just as much beside the point to come here to *be* Janet Belle Smith, that Talented, Sensitive, Lovely Person, as to come here in order to drink, insult people or make out.

The trouble is, even here people judge me apart from my work. And if I go on seeing Nick, I have to consider that they may find out and judge that. Even if nobody else notices anything, Leonard might tell Charlie, and Charlie might tell Teddy – If Teddy hasn't already guessed. Of course, he warned me against Nick the first day I was here. That story about Sally Sachs was at least partly meant as a warning ... Or was it a suggestion? Was he really talking about me as well as Ricky?

TEDDY: Overcautious technically ... costive Middle Western WASP background – well, I needn't tell *you* about that. But it's always seemed to me that a passionate affair might do him a *lot* of good ...

141

And then the other night after the races Teddy, who always stays up so late, went off to bed at ten, almost deliberately leaving us together –

If Teddy knows, he might tell Ricky, and Ricky would tell Sally. But I think if I had to I could stand that. I could bear to have Charlie know, or Gerry (he might actually approve). Anyone, really – even Caroline, though I would hate that – as long as it's not Kenneth. He must never find out.

Harmonia Waters won't know, because she left this morning after breakfast, very quietly in a taxi (compared to Anna May's departure). I was extremely sorry to see her go – the more so since I've been both too timid and too selfishly preoccupied to make friends as I perhaps might have. Gerry goes tomorrow, and I haven't really got to know him either.

But that's how it's always been when anyone leaves Illyria; even more when I leave myself. I feel as awful as I did when I was sent to camp for the first time and suddenly realized I would miss all the comic strips in the newspaper. I didn't want to go, I declared that morning. My parents thought it was for their sakes, and tried to console me with promises of letters and visits. I remember how I sobbed and sulked in the car, but couldn't bring myself to confess what was the matter: that I cared that much what would happen to Abbie and Slats, to Terry and Pat and the Dragon Lady, while I was gone. Because of course I knew already that comic strips were vulgar and foolish, and that Slats and Terry and the rest of them weren't real, and weren't even the sort of people we knew.

But I did care, very much. Just as I care whether Harmonia recovers from her operation, and Charlie starts writing again. I want to know if Gerry can get his grant renewed and go to Mexico, and if Teddy will win his copyright case against that record company.

Harmonia, Charlie, Gerry and Teddy aren't the sort of people 'we know' now. By Westford standards they are types, not people: an eccentric elderly Southern spinster, an alcoholic ex-Communist, a long-haired hippie who takes drugs, and a fat old homosexual. If I brought any of them to a Westford party, our friends would be minimally polite to them, but no more. They would also be uncomfortable with Leonard, who is obviously a New York Jewish intellectual; and gently scornful of ill-dressed, socially inept young people like Ricky and Sally. To Nick, they might not even be polite. But polite or not, they would classify all of them instantly, almost unconsciously, as types, characters – not real people.

And what's worse, *if they weren't artists,* so would I.

Kenneth, on the other hand, is 'our sort,' or rather he seems to be; which I suppose is why we became friends so fast – or seemed to. Of all the people I've met at Illyria, he's the only one I've seen socially outside. The truth is, I would feel a little uncomfortable about walking down a street in New York (let alone in Westford) with somebody who looks like Gerry or Teddy – or any of them. But that I should have let this petty snobbish self-consciousness actually prevent me from seeing them again, from becoming friends – that's awful.

After lunch

A bad scene. Or maybe it was a good scene, I don't know. I don't know anything any more.

I didn't have lunch at the pool; instead I went over to Kenneth's studio. He's made use of his sketches of Anna May, by putting her into his big new landscape, and he wanted me to see it. I wasn't awfully eager to go; not only because I felt awkward being alone with Kenneth, but because it annoyed me that he had wanted to paint Anna May, who doesn't even pose well.

KENNETH: It was hell working with her. She's a terrible model.

JANET: Is she?

KENNETH: Impossible. She can't hold a position; she yawns and sags and fidgets all the time. And though she gives such an impression of being a beauty, her features really have no character, no individual quality somehow. You can see that in the drawings.

JANET: But you went on with them all the same.

KENNETH: I felt I had to. You see, I had this weird feeling about Anna May. I still don't quite understand it. I certainly didn't want to get into bed with her, but I thought I might be in love with her in some way. I knew she was going to be terribly important to me ... Here, look at this.

I've always thought part of the mysterious attraction of Kenneth's pictures was their emptiness: the fields without cows, roads without vehicles, rooms without people. And Anna May, I would have said, was exactly the sort of thing that didn't belong in them.

But somehow this time it works. For one thing, she's almost unrecognizable. The scribbled restlessness of the sketches has been transformed into the half-presence of a female figure in the middle distance – beauty suggested by two or three lines, a patch of pink, a patch of brown. 'If she came any nearer,' Kenneth said, 'she might be ugly.' Meaning partly that her beauty is perfect exactly because it's indistinct; everyone who looks at the picture, perhaps for the next thousand years, will see what he likes. It's a good painting; Kenneth says he thinks the best he's done in a long while.

So this was all right. But then everything went wrong. We were eating chicken sandwiches and drinking iced tea, and the studio was cool and pleasant in the diffuse north light from the big window: white walls, white new-stretched and primed canvases, parallel rows of brushes and tubes of paint on the scrubbed wood table, and a parallelogram of sunshine lying on the floor by the doorway, with patterns of leaves moving in it. And then Kenneth invited me to the late show of a new movie in Jerico tonight.

But since I'd already promised to go to Nick's at ten-thirty, I had to decline. And when I did, he said at once in a peculiar thin voice, 'I thought you wouldn't come.'

I should have let it alone, but I couldn't. I began jabbering, elaborating excuses between little bites of sandwich. Kenneth, who had already finished his, didn't look up while I was talking. He sat there, smoothing out a piece of waxed paper on top of a stool and then folding it up into meticulous squares. Only whenever he said something he looked up at the end of the sentence, very briefly, as if checking the time on a clock that burnt his eyes.

JANET: It's not that I don't want to go, it's just that ...
KENNETH: Perhaps you have a previous engagement.
JANET: No, no; it's just that I don't really like spy movies, and I want to get to bed early tonight, I haven't had much sleep lately.
KENNETH: Yes, I noticed that.

This time when he glanced up his eyes were flat and pale, with reddish rims, looking hard at me through a mask made out of dry creased skin. I knew then that he suspected.

KENNETH: You've been out after midnight three nights running, you know.
JANET: Yes, I've had trouble sleeping, I've been worrying so much about my work; I've been going out for walks ...
KENNETH: I looked for you about eleven the night before last when I came back from Anna May's party; and then later when we couldn't get into Charlie's room. And again after the crisis was over. About two AM.

By this time the piece of waxed paper was the size of Kenneth's thumbnail. He put it into his black lunch box carefully and snapped the catches shut. Then he looked up and smiled, a dreadful kind of smile like a rubber band being stretched slowly.

JANET: Yes, well, I –
KENNETH: You don't have to make up any story, Janet. I know where you were. Teddy told me.

Teddy hadn't heard anything; he'd only guessed. So I could have denied it, and Kenneth might have believed me, because he wanted to believe me. But what would have been the point? He would have found out sooner or later. I didn't think any of this then; I couldn't think at all, or go on with what I was doing, which was putting the top back on my thermos, or even speak coherently.

JANET: I'm sorry – it was just that ... You see, the other day – I mean, I tried to tell you, but – I mean, the day you went to the races, and I felt so ... Really, what happened ...
KENNETH: You don't have to apologize to me. You're a free agent, after all.

What made it worse was that Kenneth wouldn't admit he minded; he just kept saying things like 'I certainly have no claim on your time,' and 'Naturally I was a little surprised,' in that same thin voice. He didn't mention Nick's name, or even refer to him – except once, when he said he had really never expected I would let myself be taken sexual advantage of by a cheap opportunist.

KENNETH: I'm afraid I've had certain illusions about you all this time. You see, I liked to think I knew someone whose life wasn't as messy and sordid as the lives of everyone else I know ... But you're just like the rest of us after all, aren't you?

If he'd only said he was furious, I could have left, or at least tried to defend myself. But since he was so calm and polite, I somehow felt I had to stay and politely go on listening to him.

And what he said then was awful. It was as if everything

he thought or knew about me – all the confidences I have ever made to him – were turned inside out and used against me.

For instance, Kenneth said that nothing but the kind of 'blameless virtue and good taste' I have been 'pretending to exemplify,' as he put it, could excuse the priggish and self-satisfied tone of not only my social behavior but my writing. Otherwise I had no right to 'sneer so very fastidiously' at the people I knew, or the characters in my stories, for their small errors – to 'delicately but firmly cast them into the pit' because they liked gladiolas, called Negroes 'Nigras,' or screamed at their children.

Which is terribly unfair, because even if I have been behaving and writing like somebody I'm really not, I didn't do it on purpose. Not only unfair: mean. But in everything Kenneth said, though he still spoke in a mild inoffensive tone, there was a kind of horrible androgynous malice I'd never heard before. (I suppose it's been there all the time, but he suppressed it as long as he thought I was Lovely Janet, so that she would think well of him.)

Then Kenneth said that it wasn't my family and friends in Westford I was trying to shield by 'not writing as honestly as you could'; it was myself.

KENNETH: Now come on, Janet. You don't really think your son's life is going to be ruined if some boys at his school know that his mother wrote a story about the facts of life. Or that your husband will lie down and die if you make fun of insurance agents. From what I've seen of him, he doesn't take either his own work or yours that seriously.

By this time Kenneth had got to the point where he was able to speak more loudly and look at me directly for as long as he pleased, with the dark spiteful glance of somebody who has decided to admit he is your enemy.

KENNETH: Oh, I grant he might be mildly annoyed. But if you want me to believe you've made this tremendous sacrifice, given up writing the truth merely for that reason –

JANET: No, no, but I want –

KENNETH: Excuse me. What you're really protecting, I think, is some idea of yourself that you're terribly fond of ... You write so well, Janet, that it's almost concealed, but your stories are full of self-congratulation and self-advertisement and self-love. They're really a form of onanism.

I never know how to meet a direct attack; am slow even to recognize one, to take in the fact that something irrevocably hostile has been said. I sat there stupidly, feeling disoriented and weightless, but stiff at the same time, as if I had just been in an auto accident.

KENNETH: What you're protecting, you see, is the idea of this charming, intelligent, sensitive lady writer who lives in a nice house in the country with her nice family, and never makes any serious mistakes or has any real problems ... You know I've always envied you, Janet. I've thought that I could have been happy and lived a decent life too, if I had a lot of money, and were married to a good man instead of a bad woman.

He actually said this. And then went on to tell me that though I have always thought he was on my side, he is really on Clark's.

KENNETH: Before I met him, I thought from hearing you talk that Clark was just a conventional, well-bred business executive. But he's much more than that. He's a very impressive man ... You may love him, for all I know; but it's obvious you haven't much respect for him, or interest in what he's really like. I've often wondered why he puts up with it.

And he recalled that day we all had lunch together in New York, when Clark began telling Kenneth about the habits of sandpipers. 'You looked so bored and superior,' he said.

148

JANET: But I've heard so much about sandpipers for so many years. Clark is always talking about how he'd like to leave the company and write a long book on bird migration.

KENNETH: Really? Why doesn't he, then?

JANET: Well, of course, because he has to support a family. He'd have to take a year off, or more, and we couldn't really afford that.

KENNETH: I thought you had investments.

JANET: Yes, we do, but —

KENNETH: You mean you *could* afford it, but you don't want to. You want to go on living in the style to which you're accustomed.

JANET: I didn't say that. You don't understand. Clark says he wants to leave his job, but that's just a way of speaking ... Really, I don't see any point in this conversation.

I tried again to put the top on the thermos, but my hands wouldn't do it, so I dropped both parts into my lunch box, shut it and stood up. I could hear the weak lukewarm tea and melted ice sloshing about inside among the sandwich crusts and orange peel. 'Well, uh, I guess I'll get back to work,' I said in a miserable, pale sort of voice.

Kenneth looked up. His face had cleared; it was as if all the black sticky spite, like molasses, had finally been poured out. He looked at me anxiously, like a human being, and said, 'Don't go. I'm sorry if I've offended you.'

I wanted to leave, but social habit was too much for me. I stood in the doorway while we exchanged some polite remarks; I agreed not to be offended and to understand that Kenneth had only spoken as he did out of his great regard for me, and to come for a drink with Teddy after dinner.

Kenneth is wrong about Clark. He would like to write a book on birds if he had the time, and maybe he will some day. After he's retired. Or even sooner if we can afford it – which we can when, as we put it, 'Fred and Patricia are gone.'

But Clark wouldn't just walk out on the company; he feels a responsibility to it, and of course to us. And besides, what would his parents say? They would say, or at least they would think, that their son was becoming mentally disturbed. Because Fred and Patricia both believe that the universal human desire is to be rich and powerful. They take it for granted in everyone, disregarding statements to the contrary, which they assume to be hypocritical. When someone's lack of ambition and greed are positively forced upon his attention, Fred calls them 'spineless' or 'neurotic.' Meaning that these people, too, covet money and power, but are psychologically unable to compete for them.

(SAVE THIS. I can't use it now, but someday ... When Fred and Patricia are gone, in fact.)

Since Clark has seldom since college done or said anything – in their presence at least – that his parents would have to recognize as contradicting their view of the world, they assume he shares it. Even if he were to tell them outright that he hates his work, they wouldn't notice, because it's more comfortable for them that way.

And it's more comfortable for me. That's what Kenneth would say. He would say that when Clark talks about leaving Westford Casualty I ought not merely to smile fondly and a little impatiently, just as I used to when Clarkie insisted he was going to the moon on the willow stump behind the garage. Instead I should take him seriously, even encourage him.

Suppose I did, and he did. What would happen? Our income would be reduced by more than half. The children would have to leave their schools (at least Clarkie would – Clary might get a scholarship). I'd have to let Bessie go, though I suppose we could afford a weekly cleaning woman, if any cleaning woman would agree to take on a house like ours by herself. The sensible thing would be to find a smaller house, with grounds that wouldn't need a gardener. And we couldn't go to New York as often, and certainly not to Mexico this winter.

Would I mind? Of course I would mind; nobody wants to live shabbily, and be condescended to by their friends. Everyone in Westford would be sincerely sorry for me because Clark had turned so peculiar; but I hate being pitied, no matter how sincerely. At first our troubles would be of great interest; they would be the latest news, and everyone would invite us to dinner more often than before to see how peculiar Clark was and how I was taking it. But soon the novelty would wear off, and we would be asked to dinner less. Our friends would begin to realize that we weren't the sort of people they knew any more, and gradually we would be dropped.

Clark wouldn't care. He doesn't care about the house, or about local society. I expect he would be off half the time anyway, making notes on some rocky shore among damp heaps of seaweed and bird droppings.

But if that's what he wants, Kenneth would say, shouldn't he have it, since it's only for one year? The trouble is, it wouldn't be only one year. If I encouraged him, Clark might leave Westford Casualty. But once he had left, I don't think he would go back, whatever I said.

So Kenneth is right.

And if he's right about Clark, what about the other things he said?

That I'm protecting myself as well as other people by not writing about certain subjects. That might be true. Of course, if Clark left the company, it would be different; I could write about insurance agents then. We might even leave Westford, and then I could write about the country club golf tournament, about Martie and Steve, about Bessie and her family, and about Julia (who doesn't scream at her children like the Julia in my story – she *whines* at them).

Yes, but even if Clark didn't leave the company, I

could write all this, and more too – if I dared. If I cared more for telling the truth than for the good opinion of people like Martie and Steve and Julia and Clark's parents. Because that's what it comes down to. ('You get what you want in life, but not your second choice.')

I don't mean I want to tell the literal truth. I don't – not because it would be too much, but because it wouldn't be enough. A writer has to alter his material – but by addition, not by subtraction as I've been doing.

The only reason for writing fiction at all is to combine a number of different observations at the point where they overlap. If you already have one perfect example of what you want to demonstrate, you might as well write nonfiction. Indeed, you *should*, because any changes made just to avoid similarity to persons living or dead, or for other extraneous reasons, are bound to be wrong.

But ordinarily you don't have a single perfect example. Instead, over the years you've noticed, say, something about the way children behave at their own birthday parties, but none of your examples is complete in itself. So you invent a children's party which never took place, but is 'realer' in the Platonic sense than any you ever attended. Fiction is condensed reality; and that's why its flavor is more intense, like bouillon or frozen orange juice.

I know all this; I've known it for years. But all the same I've begun adding water, more and more lukewarm water, to every batch I made. Because I was afraid that the un-diluted stuff would freeze and burn me, and everyone around me.

What Kenneth is wrong about is Nick. He's not a cheap opportunist, and he didn't take advantage of me, any more than I did of him. And it wasn't sordid and messy, either. It was hateful of Kenneth to say that. And he didn't say it out of a great regard for me, he said it out of jealousy and spite and disappointment. Because his Lovely Janet doesn't really exist and never did, any more than my Lovely Kenneth. They were both just ghosts in some story we were telling each other and ourselves. Very charming and spiritual, like all ghosts, but in the end thin, transparent and boring.

Lovely Janet didn't really write very well – she left too much out. She didn't want to depress her readers; she didn't want to make them uncomfortable. She didn't want to expose her family, her friends or (above all) herself; she didn't want them to be laughed at, or pitied or condemned – not even when they were in fact ridiculous, pitiable and wrong.

But it's like Nick said, when he was talking about why he put mud and broken glass into some of his paintings: you can't write well with only the nice parts of your character, and only about nice things. And I don't want even to try any more. I want to use everything, including hate and envy and lust and fear.

Not only do I want to – I must. If nothing will finally survive of life besides what artists report of it, we have no right to report what we know to be lies.

More about Penguins
and Pelicans

For further information about books available from Penguins please write to Dept EP, Penguin Books Ltd, Harmondsworth, Middlesex UB7 ODA.

In the U.S.A.: For a complete list of books available from Penguins in the United States write to Dept DG, Penguin Books, 299 Murray Hill Parkway, East Rutherford, New Jersey 07073.

In Canada: For a complete list of books available from Penguins in Canada write to Penguin Books Canada Ltd, 2801 John Street, Markham, Ontario L3R 1B4.

In Australia: For a complete list of books available from Penguins in Australia write to the Marketing Department, Penguin Books Australia Ltd, P.O. Box 257, Ringwood, Victoria 3134.

In New Zealand: For a complete list of books available from Penguins in New Zealand write to the Marketing Department, Penguin Books (N.Z.) Ltd, P.O. Box 4019, Auckland 10.

Alison Lurie

LOVE AND FRIENDSHIP

For her first novel Alison Lurie wrote about the stresses and
strains of a marriage in an American academic community.

'Alison Lurie is a writer of extraordinary talent and promise.
She is perhaps even more shocking than she knows – shocking
like Jane Austen, not Genet' – Christopher Isherwood

'Awesomely good for a first novel' – Julian Mitchell in the
Sunday Times

'The unfaltering aptness of the dialogue and the acid
penetration of the commentary provide steady, uninterrupted
delight' – Anthony Quinton in the *Sunday Telegraph*

'Very funny' – Francis Hope in the *Observer*

THE WAR BETWEEN THE TATES

Returning to a theme brilliantly expounded in her first novel,
Love and Friendship, Alison Lurie charts the miseries, the
bewilderments, the ironies – and the pleasures – that can
attack a middle-aged marriage.

'Stylish, comic detached, tender . . . she evinces rare wisdom,
wit and compassion; and she writes like an angel'
– *Sunday Times*

'Hilarious, contemporary, one of the few American novels
Jane Austen would most certainly enjoy' – Truman Capote

'Glorious in its entirety and flawless under the closest scrutiny
. . . the end result is not the championing of one cause or one
person over another, but an act of profound, compassionate and
witty understanding' – Jacky Gillott in *The Times*

'It has given me nothing but pleasure' – Francis King in the
Sunday Telegraph

Alison Lurie

THE NOWHERE CITY

Alison Lurie holds up life in Los Angeles for her ruthless inspection.

'Very rarely does one come across a novel so well constructed that it surges with life on all levels. It is a remarkably penetrating story of a city without an identity'
– *Daily Telegraph*

'The best comedy of marital relations I've read for a long time'
– *Sunday Citizen*

'Marvellous entertainment' – *Sunday Times*

'A very witty, assured, sustained creation of both people and place' – *New Statesman*

IMAGINARY FRIENDS

The Truth Seekers, a religious cult in upstate New York, may be, by and large, small-town citizens, but they do have important friends. Through their beautiful prophetess, Verena, they communicate with beings on another Planet who are soon to land on Earth in a bid to save mankind . . .

'*Imaginary Friends* is a comedy on a theme from which the Greeks made tragedies – the sin of overreach, of human beings behaving as if they were more than human . . . a comedy of ideas that stands near the top of its class' – *Life*

'Alison Lurie's most accomplished comedy . . . a beautiful, expanding metaphor for innumerable complexitities of human relationship' – *The Times Literary Supplement*

FALLING IN PLACE
Ann Beattie

It's a hot, sullen summer on America's East Coast. As John and Louise Knapp bicker at their weekend marriage; as twelve-year-old Parker makes another trip to the shrink in New York; as Cynthia the English teacher clings to her freaky lover Spangle – Ann Beattie invades Updike and Cheever territory to give us a cinematic, brilliantly comic view of America's affluent hell.

'Wonderfully funny' – *The Times*

MOTHER'S HELPER
Maureen Freely

The Pyle-Carpenter household comes complete with three children who can do what they like as long as they have Thought It Through, an intercom that never turns off, with Weekly Family Councils and with the television padlocked into a bag. Like Kay Carpenter herself, it was a totally liberated, principled, caring, warm, nurturing nucleus . . . And at first, Laura was completely fooled.

'A novel to weep over or laugh with. Whichever will stop you going mad' – *Literary Review*

DAUGHTERS OF PASSION
Julia O'Faolain

Anger, passion, tenderness . . . nine evocative stories from the author of *No Country for Young Men*. Julia O'Faolain never falters as she moves through situations both strange and familiar – the seduction of a lonely nanny in Paris, a family embarrassed by an unwelcome guest, the sharply focused memories of an imprisoned hunger-striker under pressure to eat. It is a brilliant, compulsive foray into a landscape of passion from a writer at the height of her powers.

THE MOSQUITO COAST
Paul Theroux

Allie Fox was going to recreate the world afresh. In flight
from the cops, crooks, scavengers and funny-bunnies of the
twentieth century, he abandons civilization and takes the
family to live in the Honduran jungle. There his tortured,
quixotic genius keeps them alive, his hoarse tirades harrying
them through a diseased and dirty Eden towards
unimaginable darkness and terror.

'As oppressive and powerful as its central character. It bursts
with inventiveness' – *The Times*

HOW FAR CAN YOU GO?
David Lodge

Winner of the Whitbread Book of the Year Award for 1980.

How far could they go? On one hand there was the
traditional Catholic Church, on the other the siren call of the
permissive society. And what with the advent of COC
(Catholics for an Open Church), the social lubrication of the
Pill and the disappearance of hell, it was difficult for Polly,
Dennis, Angela and the others not to rupture their spiritual
virginity on the way to the seventies . . .

'Hilarious . . . a magnificent book' – Graham Greene

A GOOD MAN IN AFRICA
William Boyd

Escapee from suburbia, overweight, oversexed . . . Morgan
Leafy is hardly overburdened with worldly success. Actually,
he is refreshingly free from it. But then, as a representative of
Her Britannic Majesty in tropical Kinjanja, it was not very
constructive of him to get involved in wholesale bribery and
with sensitive local politicians. Nor was it exactly oiling his
way up the ladder to hunt down the improbably pointed
breasts of his boss's daughter when officially banned from
horizontal delights by a nasty dose . . .

'Wickedly funny' – *The Times*